The Last Hunt

Random House
New York

The Last Hunt

Horst Stern

Translated by
Deborah Lucas Schneider

This work was originally published in German as *Jagdnovelle* by
Kindler Verlag GmbH, München. Copyright © 1989 by Kindler Verlag
GmbH, München.

Library of Congress Cataloging-in-Publication Data

Stern, Horst.
[Jagdnovelle. English]
The last hunt / Horst Stern.
    p.   cm.
ISBN 0-679-41782-6
I. Title.
PT2681.T478J3413 1993
833'.914—dc20   93-3641

Manufactured in the United States of America
98765432
First U.S. Edition

Book design by Tanya M. Pérez

The Last Hunt

In an Eastern European country, in a museum devoted to hunters and the animals they hunt, you will find displayed on one wall, on green cloth backing and under glass, the skin of a bear. Even without consulting the plaque at the bottom of the case, which mentions a year in the seventies of this century, visitors can tell that the animal was extraòrdinarily large before it was stripped of its fur. As tall as a man, with the stumps of arms and legs sticking out pathetically from the thick pelt, the skin alone is still threatening. Even as a headless trophy it makes people lower their voices as they come closer, stirs a dark ripple of fear as they imagine what the animal must have been like alive.

In addition to the date, the plaque identifies the general area where the bear was killed and the man

who killed it. The latter is a name cheerily suggestive of the Rhineland and as short as a shot. If you
expected to see a person mentioned at all, it would
be someone out of the ordinary, perhaps even the
dictator himself; the name on the plaque seems
completely out of keeping with the primitive, sha-
manistic aura of this trophy. Indeed, the only thing
that seems to go with the name is the green cloth
in the bear's shape on which someone has sewn an
ornamental border, making it look like a haus-
frau's tablecloth or one of those little paper doilies
bakers put under their cakes. Occasionally the
name prompts visitors to wonder what it costs to
get permission to shoot such an animal, as if
money were the only conceivable link between this
hunter, who couldn't have possessed very strong
magic, and his primeval kill from deep in the forest. The museum curator will say only that because
the bearskin set a record for size according to the
international formula, the man who shot it was
prohibited by law from taking it out of the country. Of course that also meant that the enormous
fee he had paid the government for permission to
kill it was returned.

The following story is about them both, the bear
and the bear slayer. Behind the words, it is true.

Joop—this was not his name—was standing at the window of his office on the top floor of a large German bank. It was late on a rainy May evening. The huge sign on the roof glowed and pulsed, flashing an optical echo of the corporation's logo onto the unbroken cloud cover in a watery blue blur. Joop was reminded that airplanes coming in to land at night create the same effect with their blinking lights when they drop through low-hanging clouds. This thought was so out of place that Joop realized he was tired; normally he did not permit his mind to stray like this.

Joop was in charge of the bank's foreign operations. When his co-workers were asked to describe him, they used words that seemed to belong to the executive floor just like the potted yucca trees in the offices and the modern paintings hanging in the halls, which the firm bought in its role as a corporate patron of the arts; they said "financial wizard," or "trend spotter," or "guru." Recently, however, an ear sensitive to nuances would have picked up a rising tone on the final syllables as Joop's colleagues offered these appraisals. It was the merest hint, of course, so faint you couldn't be sure whether it was emphasizing the message contained in the words or expressing the first seeds of doubt about their applicability to Joop. Joop was sixty.

He turned away from the window toward the dimly lighted room, a rectangle of generous size with large windows covered by skeletal blinds on one long side and three doors made of rare and expensive wood on the other. A few pieces of furniture were placed along the walls of the shorter sides. Dominating the room was a desk far too big for even the most important tasks. A huge slab of bog oak, lightly veined in gray, rested on six chrome legs forming two outward-facing triangles. On the side facing the high-backed leather desk chair, an irregular space was cut out of the desk top; this bay had been a necessary concession, disguised as if modern design, to the considerable bulk of Joop's predecessor. Such Falstaffian figures are no longer to be met with these days in the boardrooms of major corporations, however, and Joop himself, despite his thick gray hair and only medium height, had no flab on his stomach, buttocks, or thighs. No superfluous fat strained the seams of his custom-tailored suits, not even when he sat down, or made ugly sweat marks on his elegant, correctly buttoned shirts.

He tolerated the desk, having accepted it with a shrug of the shoulders when he moved into the office. It hadn't seemed terribly important, and as furniture went, it wasn't altogether without style. Besides, the cutaway space, which everyone in the building referred to as "the Bay of Pigs," served as a constant reminder to him to discipline his eating habits. He didn't use the desk for much except signing documents. His actual work was done at two small tables, which matched the style of the rest of the furniture but were actually very functional; on these stood several pieces of communications equipment and a computer. The swivel chair allowed him to shift back and forth between them quickly, and whenever either of his two secretaries entered the room from the outer office, he was almost always on the telephone or busy entering financial data onto his computer screen.

Recently, however, the two had been trading theories, more out of concern than amusement, about why they so often found him standing before a large acrylic painting, lost in thought. This distinctly strange work was Joop's personal property and the only piece of art on the walls. Framed expensively in silver, it hung at one end of the room over a black leather couch where he sometimes napped. The secretaries' theories centered on the most conspicuous element in the painting: a female figure in a flowing gown, who was painted with delicate artistry in translucent colors. An outline without depth, more of a graphic than a painterly representation of a three-dimensional figure, she was shown in a precisely executed left profile. A hand with the fingers fanned out in a mannered gesture, seemingly unattached to an arm, was lifting an exceedingly voluptuous breast, stigmatized by an erect nipple and highlighted by the livid background, out of the low neckline of a pale yellow, one-shouldered gown.

Both secretaries guessed that it was precisely this detail of the picture that attracted their employer and was causing him to linger before it until he became oblivious to all else. Their speculations were fed not only by Joop's advanced age, a time of life when, women believe, a man often becomes obsessed with erotic stimulants, but by the matter of the curtain: Since Joop's business transactions were conducted worldwide, in all different time zones, he inevitably put in some late nights at the office. In order to get some rest he had had a curtain installed; it ran on a ceiling track and could be pulled to close off the couch—and the picture—from the rest of the room. Once, when the curtain was drawn back and one of the women had come upon him staring at the picture yet again, she had looked away—turned away, in fact—and from the embarrassment in her voice as she had then delivered her message, Joop had felt sure he could guess what she was thinking. Turning toward her with a frank smile, he had launched abruptly into a little speech, saying that depicting Diana bare-breasted was purely a matter of convention, because (he added in the tone of a schoolteacher tired of explaining the obvious) that is who she was: the Roman goddess of hunting. You could recognize her from the falcon she was carrying on her right hand, and also from the sacrificial victim shown shedding its blood for her, a rather ethereal hare. The hunter offering the sacrifice to the goddess— Joop pointed to a shadowy little figure in the background—is climbing up to the terrace where Diana stands and holding in the crook of his arm the gun he has just emptied into the hare. So the breast had no real importance for the meaning of the picture, or for him personally, no matter what people might be saying.

He had blurted out this last statement without really meaning to, more from a slight amusement at the woman's discomfort than from any wish to correct the idea behind it. But then irritation had mounted in him as he heard himself delivering an impromptu lecture on a subject so totally inappropriate during business hours at a bank. This irritation, for which he had only himself to blame, had made him go on, unfairly. He had continued, rashly, when silence would have been wiser by far, humiliating this woman with whom his relationship was otherwise rather distant and marked by professional courtesy on both sides. He'd remarked that showing the detail of Diana's anatomy to which he was referring, the one that apparently gave offense to some people, could *only* be conventional, motivated by mythology, in fact, because if you considered this part of her body realistically, in purely human terms, so to speak, then for a woman of Diana's habits, who liked to go tearing around the countryside after her dogs (her other traditional companions), bouncing and jouncing over hill and dale, it would have to be, well, rather . . .

At this point he had floundered, unable to decide how to describe the possible human consequences of a goddess's athleticism. Was the right word *inconvenient,* or *uncomfortable,* or perhaps even *painful?* Each of these terms had seemed even more distasteful than the one before, and so in the end, in his eagerness to leave out nothing he could bring forward in his own defense, he had got himself hopelessly entangled. More likely, however, it had been the keen edge of his own mind, with its capacity for self-observation, that had cut off this unedifying monologue just in time. But the woman had already got the point, and muttering a hasty apology she had fled the room, covered in confusion and blushing furiously.

That had been a few weeks back, and in that moment of self-exposure and burning shame Joop had all at once realized why the picture attracted him: It *was* Diana's flesh after all, in mystical union with the blood of the hare whose life was ending as a hunter's offering, trickling away, drop by red drop. But what drew him to the picture, again and again, was above all the shadowy little man cradling the gun. From him Joop was seeking some hints of himself and of his own nature. In the hare bleeding to death he saw his own life ebbing away, and his thoughts dwelt more and more on a desire to sacrifice what was left of it to Diana.

Joop was a hunter.

He closed the curtain, switched off the light, and left his office. Dismissing the chauffeur who was waiting for him at the entrance, he set out into the night on foot. Raindrops ran down his face, and angrily, he brushed them away.

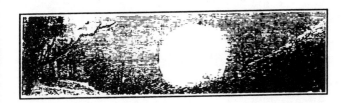

As the bear looked around for signs of danger, he was moving so fast that the sparsely covered hills rolled across the horizon and disappeared in a blur. But then it was only a bear's horizon, not very far-distant and in none-too-sharp focus to begin with. The Sioux have a saying that an eagle can see a leaf as it falls, a coyote can hear it, and a bear can smell it, and the saying existed long before the white man came with his science, his measurements and diagrams, to rob the bear of his godlike aura. But to get an impression of the world around him a bear *will* rely on his nose. This one was running along in a cloud of his own fumes, odors of cave and digestive processes that had settled in his fur during his months of hibernation. He breathed loudly through his lowered nose but he couldn't smell much other than what his high rolling gallop shook out of his shaggy fur; the wind was at his back and kept him enveloped in his own scent. Then the wind, as if uncertain from which direction it should blow, shifted through all the points of the compass and the bear suddenly caught a hint of carrion through his own reek, and a stale whiff of blood. Immediately, long threads of saliva came flowing from his jaws. He was enormously hungry. As he shook his head, the saliva dropped onto the fur of his chest and shone there like strings of pearls. It was afternoon, and the bear was running westward toward the sun, which was already low in the sky.

The scent of blood brought him up short, breaking the rhythm of his stride. When he set off again in his awkward trot, he stopped often to check the wind, settling onto his haunches and lifting his black, wet nose, which looked like a dog's. Down near the ground, where the sharp tang of thawing earth overpowered everything else, the scent of blood was too weak to follow, but it grew stronger if he raised his head. When he couldn't lift his nose any higher, the bear stood up. Dushan, who had been following the bear with binoculars since it had first cropped up among the willows on the horizon hours before, spit out the cigarette end his jittery nerves had made him mouth until it turned soggy, and the spittle sent it flying through the slit in the hunting blind. It landed and fizzled briefly in the blood-soaked patch of weeds where the young steer lay with its throat cut.

Dushan was a hunter—at least that is what he

told strangers; he even claimed to hunt bear, but everyone in his village laughed at him behind his back, because Dushan had never aimed a gun at a bear in his life and never would, unless someone's life and limbs happened to be in immediate danger. For the bears in the great forests of this part of the world were the property of the state; when they grew too old or their numbers too large, the government sold them as targets to bring in the foreign exchange of rich tourists from the West. It was Dushan's job to guide the tourists, who then shot the bears themselves—sometimes expertly, sometimes not. Usually they were excellent shots, though. It was because of their money, said the people in Dushan's village; counting it had made their trigger fingers nice and smooth.

So that was Dushan's situation, if the truth be known. He was merely the bears' state-appointed guardian, and in fact there were only two adult bears in his district, one male and a female who would soon be leaving her winter den with her two cubs. That is, Dushan expected there would be two of them. Dushan's realm consisted of bait sites where from May to October he put out food to keep the bears from killing the animals on the nearby farms. These bait sites lay far apart, because bears are unsociable and wide-ranging creatures. Depending on the season, Dushan gave them corn or potatoes, supplemented by waste from the local schnapps distilleries and, every once in a while, the meat of less-desirable domestic animals or offal from the slaughterhouse.

And if even more truth be known, he didn't

actually need a gun, except that some foreign guest for whom he was acting as guide might conceivably ignore all the regulations and blunder into a situation where a bear has no choice but to attack. That had never happened, however, for Dushan's instructions allowed the visiting hunter to shoot only from the safety of a shooting stand, an elevated blind. Any other manner of hunting a bear, such as from a truck or—heaven forbid—on foot, was strictly forbidden, under penalty of instant dismissal, in the case of the responsible game warden, and, for the hunter, the loss of his license and forfeiture of the fee paid.

It was in such a hunting blind raised off the ground on log stilts that Dushan was now sitting, after putting out the meat close by in the usual manner. The people in the Wildlife Bureau had said that the bear was supposed to grow accustomed to the bait and lose all fear of the blind next to it. For this reason, no shot could be fired from the raised platform—which wasn't all that far off the ground, actually, hardly more than nine feet— except for the purpose of killing a bear. No thought that a hunting blind right beside the bait could be dangerous should ever be allowed to form in the bear's mind. So why had the bear Dushan could now see through his binoculars stopped? Damn it all, by now the bear ought to know there was nothing to fear until the time came for it to be shot; the regulations wouldn't allow it. Dushan's impatience was prompted by the nip of the evening chill's air and by the fact that he had been sitting there since morning. He was a man with implicit faith in the wisdom of his superiors; for many years he had been an intimate witness to the lives and deaths of the bears in his district, and had seen how they, too, were governed by this wisdom. Under its judicious control they were born, fed, counted, and judged, deemed to be good or bad, chosen to live or to die, each in its appointed season as befitted a bear, and with far more profit to the country as a whole than it had cost to feed them and pay Dushan's wages. So why wasn't the bear getting a move on toward the place it was supposed to be?

But the bear remained where he was, and sniffed suspiciously to the right and left, straight ahead and back over each shoulder. He stood more than six and a half feet tall when erect, but he was so pitifully emaciated that the thick winter fur on his belly hung down in empty folds against his hind legs. He looked old and miserable. His breathing was still rapid from his run, and his breath came from his muzzle in cheerful white puffs against the cold May air. Otherwise there was nothing cheerful about this bear. The powerful paws on his shaggy front legs were slowly going up and down in an alternating motion Dushan had seen wrestlers make as they circled each other warily in the ring. As he stood, the bear urinated in spurts that betrayed his inner agitation, but even without seeing this Dushan had known the animal was a male.

Probably he was not the bear Dushan had been waiting for, however, the one he knew from previous years and for whom he had put out the steer carcass. Suddenly he was absolutely sure of this. He set down his binoculars, which a wealthy German hunter had given him some years before in thanks for guiding him to an especially fine buck. Glancing down quickly at the ladder leading up from the ground—it was not a long one—he immediately fixed his gaze on the bear again and began to grope around with one hand for his gun. As he touched it, he realized his hand was trembling. It had been a long time since the sight of a bear had unsettled him so.

The twilight sucked the bear in and erased him from the visible world. A strong south wind had come up; it ripped the thick cloak of cave odors lingering around the bear's body, carrying it away in stinking scraps toward the North, where the bear had come from. The rain that followed soon soaked him to the skin; his winter sleep seemed to have robbed him of fat everywhere, even from his fur. He seemed to have lost everything: his form to the darkness, his smell to the wind, and his strength to the small death of a long sleep. Wearily he lay and licked his front paws, which were worn and cracked from his travels, two years of wandering on his way back from exile in a distant, alien country to the place where he had been born. He had been driven away from home after repeatedly losing fights, the last three in succession, with other male bears over females and territory. Repelled again and again at the boundaries of their territories, prevented from mating and covered with festering bite wounds, he had retreated farther and farther north in those long-ago days, until he found some peace and quiet in a remote valley in the Alps.

Now he was returning.

He had lost those fights, despite his powerful muscles and the natural courage arising from his great size, because he was unwilling to accept any of the bait sites, of which there seemed to be as many in his home country as there were bears. The smell of human beings seemed to linger in the bushes and trees around these places, and that kept him away, although the others gobbled greedily enough, oblivious to all else. And because in his youth he had once almost been thrashed to death in a sheep pen and had not forgotten it, he stayed away from farm animals as well. And so, apart from the rare find of a new litter of still-blind rabbits, he was reduced to a vegetable diet, with a mouthful of wild honey now and then. What he lacked was a kind of aggressiveness, a nastiness that nature does not ordinarily demand of a bear but that becomes necessary when food is conveniently delivered to the same place every day and must be defended. This bear wasn't greedy or mean enough; *he wasn't enough of a vicious swine.* He didn't know this. He had simply left. Back then he had emigrated to that Alpine valley, where for many years it was quieter. Recently, however, men had brought in their noisy machines and begun to build a dam across the river. He had moved on again. And now he was home.

He lay in the rain, moaning softly, his fur parted on his back and pasted to his skin as if with gel, surrounded by a large black puddle made audible by the pattering drops. He was cold. His heartbeat slowed again; winter was still in his blood. The urge to sleep came over him, but out here in the open he kept himself awake, as caution dictated, by rocking backward and forward. It was these rhythmic pulsations, passing from legs to body, that were turning his normally steady growl into this undulating moan. The wind had swelled into a storm, a booming organ to which the bear might have been singing a descant. But the rain, blowing almost horizontally now, drowned out the song with its hiss, so that soon the bear fell silent. He turned onto one side, expelled a few sounds like sighs, and then fell asleep. After a while his four legs began to make walking motions, slowly at first, awkwardly, then faster and more regularly, so that his paws splashed up the water in the puddle as they churned. The moans started up again, high and sharp now and interrupted by short intervals of panting: The bear was dreaming. What he was dreaming of no one can know.

A great silence woke him and quickly brought him to his feet, front legs first, to sharpen his senses, then the back legs. There was silence because the rain had stopped, and the wind had blown itself out. Disoriented, the bear sniffed at the departing weather front and found himself looking at a broken sky, with an almost full moon shining through the sailing scraps of clouds. He stood with his legs wide apart and shook the dripping fur around his ribs. Showers of spray sparkled in the moonlight. Loud smacking sounds, made by the fur slapping back and forth, accompanied the dance of the thousand droplets, as if an invisible audience were loudly applauding an especially good performance. The noise frightened a doe, who emerged from a nearby willow thicket and fled in long, high bounds. The bear had no difficulty finding the bed she had just left. In it lay, so newly born it was still wet, a trembling fawn. The bear sniffed it, grunted contentedly, and killed it with one bite above its fragile spine. It was his first taste of meat in a long while.

The next day the bear took the yellow light of the rising sun on his back and set off with it toward the West. He had no particular reason for choosing to trot in this direction, unless it was the feeling that the growing warmth of the morning light dried his fur best, from three sides at once. His gait was flat-footed, with his front paws turned inward; rosy drops fell on them from his lowered muzzle as he loped along. Greed had sent saliva flowing freely as he devoured the newborn fawn, and now, mixed with his victim's thin blood, his spittle had turned pink and given his slightly gaping maw a murderous appearance. He stopped and licked the spittle from his paws, but this was not really what made him want to put his feet into his mouth. It was his claws. During his winter sleep they had grown into long, ivory-colored curved daggers, and a few short walks up and down in front of his den had not been enough to wear them down. Now they hurt when he trod on a stone or knocked up against an exposed tree root; he felt the pain where they pushed up into his flesh.

With an ill-humored growl he threw himself onto his side and pulled at the claws, first one, then another. This gave him some relief, but when he got up and set out again, the pain came back. His growl grew shriller and angrier. He eyed the line of trees to his right, where the forest started; he had been running parallel to it for some time, and now he altered his course to go diagonally toward it. In front of the first row of trees, where winter storms had created gaps like missing teeth, there was a broad strip of bushes, a thicket of goat willow mixed with some hazel and elder shrubs. It was so high he couldn't identify for certain the peculiar odor wafted across it by a light breeze. Relying on his strength, he hunched his head down between rounded shoulders, shut his eyes, and broke through it in a few giant leaps. The impetus this gave him was necessary, too, for the thick-branched bushes stood arm in arm. At the end of the last bound he was suddenly standing in a road.

Even before looking around for danger signs, he instinctively raised his paws to his mouth; his landing on the road had pushed his claws up into his flesh, making them more painful than ever. But now they gave off a vile and biting stench that rose into his nostrils, and he recoiled with a terrified growl. He had never smelled anything like it before. And because he had learned to associate every new and strange odor with humans, his first impulse was to flee. But when he tried, to his horror, he found himself caught in something like stiff glue, so that he could pull his feet free only one at a time, with great effort.

There had been a pothole in the road, opened by the frost and widened by traffic, and the bear had jumped into the large patch of fresh tar mixed with gravel that had been used to fill it.

His last bound had carried him out of the goat-willow thicket into another world, a world whose natural shapes began to shed their skins like vipers. In the bear's experience this process made snakes slow and vulnerable, and the bear could catch them. But while a snake that has molted remains recognizable to a bear's eyes and nose, the world here had emerged as a violent onslaught of images and odors. It was enough to make a bear lose courage, since it hemmed in his existence and forced him to live within ever-smaller circles, turning in on himself again and again in the hope of meeting something familiar at last. It is the continual recurrence of the known that enables the present to be pure and undisturbed; it is the good fortune of creatures who live far from man.

With an unmistakable air of disgust, the bear limped stiffly across the road and into the forest on the far side. The soles of his stinking, sticky feet were soon covered with brown needles fallen from the spruce trees that grew thickly here, their branches bare to just below their intertwined tops. He tried to shorten his claws and rub his paws clean on a trunk, but it was covered with resin, so he had to give up and go on through the spindly spruces, deeper and deeper into the forest. He was looking for a more open stand of smooth, silvery beeches with trunks so thick that even a strong bear could not make their leaves shake. As he went on, a strange rushing and roaring noise grew louder, of a kind no wind could make, no matter how strong. It swelled and ebbed in a rhythm the bear could not account for, rising to a howl, ceasing for the space of a few breaths, and then starting in again. He kept going toward the roaring sound until the scraggly trees thinned out and he could see another road beyond the last of them, not very far ahead. But this road was utterly different from the one he had crossed not long before with such deplorable consequences for his feet. This one was the color of snow, although no snow lay on it; that much he could smell. Sunlight flickered across it, obscuring its far side; it was so broad that seen through the bear's eyes the opposite side almost merged with the sky. Blurred objects were passing in large numbers; their speed in both directions was such that their outlines turned into streaks of noise. Never before had the bear seen anything even remotely similar, and what he saw, heard, and smelled alarmed him. It drove him back into the spruce forest.

He trotted westward again, the old road to his left, the new one to the right, perilously close to both, but he had no choice. Small sharp-edged stones stuck to the tarry needles under his feet and dug into his flesh. And so when he came to a brook, he flung his maltreated paws out and shook them, one after the other and again and again, as if he were having convulsions. In this way he succeeded in shaking off the worst of the clumps, although a coating of tar remained. When he had finished, he stood indecisively for a while, his vacant eyes seeming to look inward. You might have guessed he was thinking, and the small cloud of insects dancing above his head could have been his unsettled thoughts.

Finally, after testing the bank with his front paws to see if it was slippery, he climbed into the slow-moving and rather shallow brook. As he eyed his reflection, he was startled to see the water around him taking on an iridescent shimmer. It was suddenly covered with a fine skin, just as paper-thin, smooth, and multicolored as those he found between the hide and flesh of the rabbits he occasionally caught. Only this skin on the water was growing bigger and bigger; it spread to touch both banks without tearing, and one end began to float slowly downstream while the other still encircled his body.

Sniffing this skin curiously, he found himself smelling—weakly but unmistakably—his own tarry paws, even though they were now planted on the bed of the stream. This discovery sent him scrambling up the bank, where he stood, shivering, with the water running off his belly and legs. It was not from the cold of the water. These shivers came from his terrified heart and spread to his mouth, where they shook his lower jaw. Now the tangle and disorder of his fur had spread to his meager thoughts.

Joop lived alone. Two marriages had failed, and a few other liaisons as well. Each time the minimal infatuation had been lacking that carries a relationship beyond the desire to undo buttons and hair. Having a wife had simply seemed part of the game—although of what game, Joop couldn't exactly say. The game of life, maybe, an answer roughly equivalent to shrugging his shoulders. It didn't require using his head. The end was always only a question of money, a matter he left to his lawyers. Once, in a cabin in the mountains, as he and a fellow hunter were drinking to the successful kill of a stag, he had allowed his host to inquire about his feelings in these relationships with women, and in a sudden burst of inspiration whose distance from the topic at hand surprised even him,

Joop had compared them to the thermodynamic principle of entropy. By simply living our lives, Joop had said (more or less), by using up feelings, consuming the material essence of the universe, we contribute to a constant increase of disorder in the places where matter is stored, whether we like it or not. Meaning in our hearts and minds too, he had added after a short pause in which he tried to recall the article he had read some time before and what it had actually said. For according to quantum theory (he repeated these glittering words and followed them up with a mouthful of equally impressive phrases), according to quantum theory the biochemical engrams of mental processes stored in the brain do not differ in any way from objects we are accustomed to consider as material.

At this point he had felt a bit like Icarus when his wings began to melt—but not because he was in any doubt about the correctness of his last remark. (Joop had got a high return on the time he invested reading the philosopher-physicists Heisenberg and Weizsäcker and the biochemist Prigogine.) It was instead that had his companion pressed for further details, Joop would have been plunged into rather deep waters. He made a mental note (like one of the question marks he put in green ink on the margins of documents at the bank) to look up the second law of thermodynamics when he got home: *The entropy of the universe tends to a maximum,* something like that. He had also begun to feel the effect of the alcohol. And so for a moment he had been tempted simply to stop short, to feign a yawn, perhaps, and point out the lateness of the hour. But he loathed leaving unfinished any undertaking he had embarked upon; it was a point he felt strongly about, whether the undertaking was a business deal, an affair with a woman, or a train of thought on a subject of some importance. The central metaphor of Joop's life was his big, empty desk. Any untidiness, any unfinished business there, reminded him of a wild animal that a hunter has taken poor aim at and failed to kill. It has fled, wounded, and because you have no dog along to follow its trail, you have no way to put it out of its misery. Joop always had a dog along: his own short-haired self-discipline, which kept right on his heels and leapt into action at the prompting of a mere thought, wagging its tail, to correct the bad shots that not even a Joop could avoid every time.

And so it was on that occasion as well; he had finished taking out all the garbage that had collected in his emotional household (which was how he now thought of his long monologue that night) and made quite a respectable job of it, too, considering the time and place. Entropy, he had gone on to say, which is a measure of the disorder created by such irreversible processes, entropy is thus constantly increasing. And when the end comes—no one can say when—it will be as a kind of lukewarm super-meltdown, the establishment of a final equilibrium and homogeneous temperature throughout the aggregate material of the universe, which our actions will have turned into garbage. And on this garbage heap—this is a particularly important point—will be language as well, the words we use to express our feelings. On the other hand, Joop said, bringing his flight across difficult territory to a landing, on the other hand such a maximization of entropy might not necessarily mean the physical end of everything, since as far as my personal universe of garbage is concerned, I could by now have put an end to its lukewarm homogeneity several times.

Testing the aftertaste left by this remark, Joop felt it hadn't been what you would call the strongest possible finish. To make up for it he had raised his empty glass to his companion and with an irony directed at nothing in particular actually uttered that unspeakable word, *tallyho!* He needn't have bothered, as his host had already nodded off, worn out by the shifting paradigms of entropy in Joop's inner and outer worlds. Joop had taken his rifle and tiptoed out into the breaking dawn. Climbing onto a shooting stand in the first rays of light, he shot a large male fox he saw stalking a drowsy young doe that had been left alone by its mother. He recalled having felt good after that.

Now, thinking about that long-past night on his way home from the bank, he could remember the good feeling but not the reason for it. He had not pulled the trigger out of any suspicion that the fox might have rabies, of that he was sure, nor was there any need to protect a doe in that district, where the deer population was too large, like everywhere else, and was interfering with the natural regeneration cycle of the forest by eating all the young trees.

No, thought Joop as he unlocked his front door, probably the reason I felt so good afterward is that it was such a good shot (the fox had been killed instantly).

Inside the apartment he found a special-delivery letter waiting for him, placed neatly in the middle of his otherwise empty desk by the maid. It was from a Dushan someone-or-other (a last name with so many consonants in it that Joop could neither pronounce it nor read it properly). Joop recalled having used a hunting guide with that name, a man just this side of fifty with Slavic features and a cigarette stuck permanently in his unshaven face, dressed in the inevitable cloth cap of the socialist worker and cheap department-store clothes that reeked of stale smoke. As thanks for leading him to a 12-point buck on a trip to Eastern Europe some years back, Joop recalled, he had given this Dushan his old night binoculars, since he had noticed the man could hardly take his eyes off them.

Joop was uneasy. How had this faraway guide discovered his home address, and what did he propose to tell him now that he had? Joop turned the envelope with its awkward handwriting back and forth, wavering. Finally he laid it, unopened, back on the desk, but immediately picked it up again, as if compelled by some new thought, and carried it to a chest of drawers. It might have seemed by this peculiar changing of location as if Joop were trying to dismiss the no-doubt-entropic letter from his orderly life, unread. Whatever the case, that night he slept badly.

I hope you remember me, sir, and I am still

taking good care of the beautiful binoculars you were kind enough to give me. In appreciation I am writing now to tell you that a bear has been sighted in the vicinity that might appeal to you. I have seen it myself, and it is very big and so old that I am sure the Wildlife Bureau will be willing to sell it. No one has ever seen this bear here before, and if you are interested in trying to get permission to hunt it, there is no time for delay. If the bear cannot approach the bait sites, because they are claimed by other bears, then it may become aggressive and attack the farmers' livestock, which is not allowed and certainly against the law for the bear, which is why the Bureau may be willing to sell the rights to it this year, through the agency that sold you the roebuck a few years ago. I'm sure you remember, and that you also know how long these things can take. I just wanted to let you know about this, in return for your kindness, and also to suggest that you might ask for me as your guide if permission to shoot the bear is actually given. But please, sir, if I may ask you a favor, don't mention to anyone that I was the person who told you about this bear. Just submit a normal application to go bear hunting, and I will make sure that everything else is OK. . . .

This is how Joop translated the rather garbled and awkward German of Dushan's letter, moving his lips as he read it, like someone savoring a spicy new ingredient or two in an otherwise familiar soup. Studying it in the backseat of the car on his way to the bank, he was amused, and for a moment considered taking the man up on his suggestion. Then he came to the slangy "OK" and angrily crumpled up the letter in an abrupt gesture. The chauffeur, puzzled, and not conscious of having made any mistake in his driving, glanced into the rearview mirror. But Joop already had himself in hand again. It had been that awful Americanism, that word that always made him think of a wad of chewing gum being masticated in a giant, cowlike jaw. But a word alone wouldn't have set off such a vehement reaction; it was also that this slack-jawed abbreviation, a distillation of everything Joop loathed about casual American manners, seemed nowhere more out of place than spoken in connection with the hunt. Joop held on to this purist attitude despite the painful embarrassment he regularly felt when forced to participate in the arcane rituals of his fellow huntsmen or, even worse, to endure the gamy taste of the sport's over-ripe jargon on his own tongue. In his opinion, an expression like "OK" was flagrantly lacking in the respect a hunter owed to any wild animal, let alone, as in this case, a bear. For what separated a hunter from a butcher if he killed an animal with no regard for its dignity, in cold blood and a mur-derous flow of small talk?

But then Joop smoothed out the letter again and put it into his attaché case, which lay open next to him on the seat. There, on top of a pile of impor-tant bank documents, it looked like a battered old savings book that had strayed into a collection of gold certificates. Joop had a keen sense for dissonances, and while he was aware that they might be portents of the future, he liked to see their humorous side. Irony took away their symbolic force, made them easier to digest intellectually. And so with a trace of returning good humor he attributed his momentary irritation to the dissonance between the dark gray flannel of his business suit and the loden green of his thoughts. Besides, the annoying letter even reminded him of something extremely pleasant: The very next day he was due to fly to the States, to attend a World Bank hearing in New York. They would be discussing the advisability of granting further loans to nations already in danger of defaulting on previous ones. Among these countries were one or two in Eastern Europe.

The bear recovered from his fright in a hole, partly covered with large pieces of abandoned metal, where there was nothing to gnaw on but the tree roots he scratched out of the earthen walls. Then, at long last, he found the right tree for scraping his paws clean: a tall, medium-size ash with no gummy resin on its trunk. The tree stood downstream from the place where the bear had seen the water change color, and it rose above its surroundings, a pitiful crowd of bushes, like a king above his subjects. The ground was too damp for pines here. The bear pulled himself up to his full, impressive height on this ash tree and tested the strength of the bark by digging his long claws into its vertical grooves, cautiously at first and subsequently with more force. When he saw that the bark offered enough resistance, he gave a satisfied grunt and began ripping the bark with his claws, in long, downward strokes that intensified to a fury and did not stop for a long time. This abuse soon reduced the bark to shreds, leaving bare wood and bleeding sap. As the bear rubbed the tar-smeared soles of his feet against this, it immediately turned black, as if the tree's wounds had been attacked by instant gangrene. The flesh under his claws began to sting, and he dropped to all fours with a dull thud and sat back onto his haunches. Next he gripped the tree lower down with his front paws and rocked back and forth on his rump, rubbing first his left and then his right rear paw on an uninjured part of the trunk. He kept at this for a long time. The procedure was awkward, but such cleaning was seldom necessary, although after a while it produced satisfactory results. The bear inspected his four paws, sniffing and licking, and then rolled forward onto all fours. He rubbed one flank against the trunk of the ash tree, but he seemed distracted and in ill humor. His guts were growling from hunger. He urinated and set out again, in a westerly direction, to walk his rumbling stomach into silence. Hunger kept him company.

The bear was dragging a long shadow behind him when he finally emerged from the forest into an open, unplanted field reflecting raindrops in the last rays of the sun. The roads had finally taken their leave of him, the old one veering off to the south and the new one to the north. The sun crawled into a dingy yellow bed of clouds on the horizon; it was the color of his urine and promised more wetness to come. Night was approaching, the bear's second since he had returned to his home district, and the events of the day had made it seem even more unfamiliar than it should after an absence of many years. He stopped and tore at some dry, bristly grass with his long teeth, grazed along the edge of a last remaining patch of dirty snow, slaked his thirst by licking for a long time at the cleaner white snow near the ground, ate some more grass, licked more snow, and uncovered the cadaver of a thrush. Taking it in his front paws, he plucked it mostly clean with his teeth and spit the feathers out. The pitiful morsel that remained once the feathers were gone went down his throat in one gulp.

He lay down in the snow. Hunger burned in his vitals and sent a wave of heat through him. It couldn't be the thrush making him feel warm; he hadn't yet digested it, and besides, the bird was too small. Nor could it be the bird making his breath so foul. It was almost as if the few bites of fawn, thrush, and grass he had swallowed had not stirred his stomach to life after the winter months of hibernation but had simply started to rot instead. He stank now in three different ways; his fur and his breath reeked, and the smell of his paws was not much improved. From far away, the faint neighing of a horse reached his ears, and a dog, also far off, began to howl. A deer barked hoarsely from a clump of trees; close by, a mother fox yapped at her kits, urging them into their den; from somewhere came the hollow sound of a hare thumping the ground. Startled by the commotion, a late-flying crow cawed, and a horned owl hooted from a stand of fir trees. A shifting wind carried far and wide the news that a bear had emerged from his winter lair with guts stinking from hunger.

The bear lay without moving. He would have to wait until the evening breeze that was slowly rising began to blow steadily out of the West, driving his odor into the fir trees behind him and clearing the air toward the horizon; then he would be able to set out into the wind in search of the foxes' den or a litter of young hares hiding in the grass. As the last light faded he got up and trotted back under the cover of the firs, lay down again with his head on his paws, and watched darkness spread over the open country. From the horizon, near the place of the horse's neigh and dog's howl, a light appeared. It was not a star. The bear sniffed the air, more out of habit than alarm, but it offered no clues to his nose. By the time the light started to come toward him, he had already fallen into a light sleep.

Joop had been to New York. Now he was back at the Bay of Pigs, starting the report the board would expect from him about the hearings he had attended there. He was dictating it into a small tape recorder. After an opening remark to his secretary about the highly confidential nature of what was to follow, he instructed her to type it double-spaced to leave room for editing, and listed the people who should receive copies of the finished document. A pause followed, and as it began to seem too long to impose on the steadily churning tape, he switched it off. He considered blaming his hesitation on the recent transatlantic trip; sometimes flying from one time zone to another left him unable to concentrate. But he rejected the idea as soon as it occurred to him. Jet lag might increase the ambivalence that was now threatening to paralyze him, but its real cause lay in a professional dilemma that he had become more acutely aware of over the years: Joop lived simultaneously with two different incarnations of truth. Intellectually he accepted both; opportunistically he deceived each one with the other. As a rule he was unfaithful to the ecological truth, which did after all exist, in favor of the economic truth (because this was the rule in the business world, like wearing gray flannel; it was serious and useful and expected of him). But occasionally he cheated on the economic truth to sneak out with the ecological one (because a hunter did that now and then, just as he wore loden green; it was also serious and useful and expected of him). Now, however, it was time for business as usual.

In New York, Joop had foreseen a new outbreak of his dilemma. Pulling up in his limousine to the Chase Manhattan Plaza, where the World Bank sessions were being held, he found himself faced by the usual three dozen or so demonstrators who invariably picket international finance conferences. They held up their placards for him and the other arriving bankers to see. DOLLARS & POUNDS ARE THE RICH MAN'S HOUNDS, Joop read, noting with some admiration that the slogan was intellectually, or poetically, a cut above average. The sign next to it was perhaps even better: SWISS FRANCS AND MARKS ARE THE RICH MAN'S SHARKS. Of course there had also been the obligatory FUCK YOU, and the placard DEUTSCHE MARKS ÜBER ALLES was probably intended for his benefit; the previous evening several TV stations had run an item about his arrival for the sessions, with a shot of his face. In Joop's opinion some of the protest was fairly witty, and the word *rabble,* which usually came to mind when he confronted street demonstrations, had not occurred to him this time. Perhaps it was because the crowd included a black trumpet player with fat Dizzy Gillespie cheeks, performing the old number "With Plenty of Money and You" ("They say money is the root of all evil . . .") Joop liked this kind of slightly commercialized jazz. And as he made his way through the protesters to the entrance, two of them held out their hands palms up, as if asking for money, saying, with broad grins: *Thanks for nothing, big spender!* The crowd was still laughing as he entered the lobby, where several bank employees greeted him with polite apologies for the disturbance and escorted him to his seat on the podium in the conference room.

The sessions were tiring, the same old things he had been hearing for years: The representatives of the poor countries spoke volubly of an approaching dawn, a rosy glow rising on the horizon after a long and dark financial night, and the emissaries of the rich countries took this to be merely a reflection of how deeply their already huge accounts were sinking into the red. Hope was met by fear, and often enough the emotions switched sides, as the have-nots' hopes for new loans turned to fears that they would be buried in an avalanche of interest they already owed, and the haves' fears about the old loans were soothed by hopes of miracles the new loans would be able to work. The room hummed with many conversations in many languages, but this was not the only reason Joop felt reminded of Brueghel's painting of the Tower of Babel. In his drifting thoughts the Tower had transformed itself into an image of the world on the eve of the Apocalypse, a monstrous edifice of debt with all of mankind imprisoned inside and fault lines of inflation running right under its foundations, sending up seismic shocks until its walls burst. For those who had eyes to see, the figure of Reason was visible escaping through the cracks.

Joop's thoughts took him back to the demonstrators outside the bank. Surprised that his own reaction to them had been so mild, he was tempted to give it a religious interpretation, an analogy to the biblical image of the Apocalypse, and to conclude that the hatred of money expressed out there had had something Franciscan about it. For on closer inspection the hatred hadn't been directed so much at money itself as at a use of it that condemned the majority of mankind to acute poverty. According to legend, Joop recalled, Saint Francis once found a bulging purse in the street, and his discovery of a snake inside was the story's way of pointing out the evil effects of money.

Having arrived at this point in his thoughts, Joop hastily switched on the tape recorder and dictated a report that did not veer off on questionable sidetracks, reaching the conclusion that the debtor nations listed in Appendix 1 should not be denied further financial support for their development schemes, if only for the sake of maintaining their ability to pay interest on previous loans. (Joop had already culled this list from his notes and files during the return flight, accompanying the dry figures with a dry champagne.) The countries seeking further loans still had considerable natural resources, and these, in his opinion, represented sufficient collateral. Although the bank consortium could not seize them directly, it could acquire the rights to develop and exploit them. For these reasons and subject to the board's approval, he had concurred . . . Here Joop reversed the tape and inserted the words *of course* after the word *approval,* making it: For these reasons and subject to the board's approval, of course, he had concurred with the vote of the consortium members in favor of the proposed measures. The vote was, as usual, unanimous.

Going through his notes one more time before dictating Appendix 1, Joop paused at the description of a highway planned through a certain region of an Eastern European country. One of the places named had seemed vaguely familiar as he read through the loan application on the plane, but the usual row of unpronounceable consonants had kept him from giving it further thought. Now that he had to spell some of these foreign place-names for his secretary, the reason he might have recognized it suddenly struck him. His attaché case lay open on the desk to his left, and he fished Dushan's letter out of it. The name of the town it had been sent from was identical to one along the proposed route of the new highway, which was essential, or so the country's loan application claimed, for the development of tourism.

Joop held the letter in his hand for a while, thinking. Then at last he put it back into his case and closed the lid gently, as if he were trying to lock away, silently and securely, unwelcome thoughts about being unfaithful to one of his truths.

Dushan, walking along beside the cart, spoke soothingly in his deep voice to calm the horse. Then, feigning calmness himself, he stepped forward and grasped the short rope knotted to the harness. That would be the best way to prevent the horse from bolting and possibly overturning the two-wheeled cart it was pulling, laden with the fresh carcass of a donkey. The night was still and the path easily visible in the moonlight as Dushan had set out from the cabin that served as the game warden's station. He had reckoned with an uneventful trip to the bait site and not bothered to tie the meat down securely. He had also extinguished the cart's hissing gas lamp, which was keeping him from hearing the sounds of the night, and thrust it through a hole in the filthy tarpaulin he had thrown over the dead donkey. When the horse began to snort and throw back its head, showing the whites of its eyes in the moonlight, Dushan at once thought of the bear.

The horse stopped in its tracks and pawed the ground, trembling. Dushan cooed to it throatily and pulled on the halter, but to no avail. With a violent twist the horse broke loose and hurled itself in the direction they had come from, dragging both man and cart with it, then let out a terrified whinny and reared so sharply that the carcass slid off the open-sided cart and landed in the path with a thud. In its panic the animal got its hind legs caught around one of the shafts and then entangled in the harness, overturning the cart and pitching it on top of the donkey. Thrown off balance, the horse broke down, hindquarters first, then the forelegs. It lay on its side, kicking out wildly; one hoof beat against the cart, another pierced the cadaver's swollen belly. At last it lay still, dazed with fear, only its flanks heaving as it gasped for breath, snot pouring from its nostrils. A burst of foul-smelling gas escaped from the cadaver with an obscene belch, making the silence of the surrounding forest almost palpable. That a bear might approach them from behind, with the wind carrying its pungent predator's scent to the terrified horse, was something Dushan hadn't reckoned with.

When the cart tipped over and pulled the horse down with it, a black silhouette was suddenly visible against the brighter sky, revealing to the bear the presence of a man who until then had blended into the shapeless mass of moving shadows. The bear turned tail and ran, sped on his way by the crack of a shot behind him.

The scent of meat, both fresh and putrid, had roused him from his doze under the spruces at the forest's edge. Hastily he got to his feet. He had been only half asleep, in that state where his awareness was dimmed but not cut off from his surroundings; some part of him continued to register the sounds and smells through which the world presents itself to a bear. By now the wind was blowing steadily and evenly toward him, so that even without the alluring scent of flesh it bore, the time would have come to get up and venture out into open territory, to do something about the hunger still gnawing at his entrails.

At this point the bear was still unknowing about the kind of prey that was approaching, and its route; there was flesh, both dead and living, hints of leather and canvas, something gassy, too, that didn't seem to be coming from the carrion, and an odor of sweat too fine for a horse—all mingled together in a filmy cloud. He began to investigate in the usual manner, moving around its edges to learn more about what the night was sending his way. With every sense sharpened and directed toward his left and the promising, odoriferous cloud, he began to circle around, staying right on the borderline where the scent trailed off, stopping now and then to make sure of its progress. When at last he reached the point in his circuit where the moonlight was with him, he could make out the outline of a horse pulling a cart. Only experience, which had taught that where there is a horse, a human will usually not be far away, kept him from moving in swiftly to attack. But now, uncertain, he held off and continued to move around the rim of the meaty cloud, poking his open, greedily salivating muzzle into it and moving his jaws, as if he had already arrived at his meal. This was how he finally came to the rear of the little convoy. As the wind was blowing directly away from him here, the scent grew faint, and the hunger that had driven him to follow his nose blindly caused him to come so close to the horse that it shied, panicked at bear scent strong and alien enough to penetrate the smell of the carcass, as rancid bacon will cut through the taste of even the gamiest venison.

After he had fired the warning shot into the air, Dushan put the safety catch on his rifle, propped it against the carcass, and began to unhitch the trapped and still-trembling horse. With a curse he pulled it to its feet. A hard slap on its rump and a sharp command sent the frightened animal off at a gallop; Dushan knew from experience that it would make straight for home and its stable, in the village a few miles beyond the game warden's station. The risk that the bear would attack it on the way was, in Dushan's opinion, virtually nil. Without a load to pull, the galloping horse would be too fast for the bear, and besides, the shot must have prompted it to return to the shelter of the forest. The donkey had to be left where it was, however.

It was far too heavy for Dushan to lift back onto the cart by himself.

He took a moment to consider the situation and decided to take up a position at a safe distance from the carcass, where he could wait to see whether the bear would return to it. By *safe,* he said to himself emphatically, he meant a place where the direction of the wind would not give him away to the bear; he was not making any admission of fear. About two hundred paces away he found a mound of small boulders, about as tall as a man, piled up by farmers who had cleared them from nearby fields now long-abandoned. The mound offered some protection and, if he climbed it, a good view and a clear shot in every direction, in case he had to shoot the bear in self-defense. The strong night binoculars the German gentleman had given him would allow him to identify the animal for sure, even in the dark, but Dushan had been in no doubt for some time now that the bear responsible for his present predicament was the same one he had seen coming over the horizon unexpectedly not long ago, when he was sitting on the shooting stand. Holding up a hand to shield the match, he lit a cigarette and hid its quivering glow behind the rocks. That his hand was trembling he chalked up to the effort it had cost him to pull the fallen horse to its feet, even though he had noticed the same tremor on his first encounter with this bear.

Each now knew about the other, and since each feared the other, the main battle each had to wage was with himself. The bear struggled with the hunger that goaded him to return to the carcass at once, and Dushan fought with a night creeping along so slowly that he was finding it difficult to carry out his duty. This, he knew, was to prevent the bear from becoming attached to this spot, far from one of the bait sites sanctioned by the regulations. If it found meat here it would stay for days, becoming a threat to both man and livestock. A bear was never more aggressive than when disturbed in the middle of a meal on a nice piece of carrion.

The bear had retreated under the cover of the spruces, but he had taken the scent of the meat with him from the encounter and now refused to let it go. With his moist and sensitive nose he followed every slight shift of the night wind and the corresponding rise or fall in the odor's intensity, moving to the right or left with the wind if it showed an inclination to veer. He took care to set his paws down softly and not to inhale the sweetish odor of putrefaction too loudly. The rest of the mixture was not good: the human smell, and the smoke that came from no kind of fire the bear had experienced. The strength and blend of odors told him something he already knew from his quick retreat to safety under the trees: The sources of both his desire and his fear were not far off. Two conflicting urges struggled within him in a battle that intensified until it broke out on the surface and his head, neck, and shoulders began to rock back and forth as if his whole upper body were following the motion of a nervous pendulum. His front paws shifted noiselessly on the soft bed of pine needles.

To Dushan, who could see it clearly through his binoculars, the bear appeared to be doing a kind of Indian war dance. It had come forward out of the shadows to the edge of the forest, drawn by the smell of carrion as clearly as if there had been a ring through its nose with a rope attached. The sight was beautiful and fearsome in equal measure. As Dushan looked through the lenses, they cut out the trees, which could have put the bear's size in true perspective, and suddenly brought the beast terrifyingly near. The sight aroused a storm of the most contradictory emotions. While he felt pride at standing his ground despite the danger, his fear of remaining in such an alarming place was mounting rapidly. When the bear at last began to come closer, a moving black threat that almost filled the binoculars, Dushan let go of them, reached for his gun, unlocked the safety in nervous haste, and fired above the bear's head. The bullet must have ricocheted off a tree, to judge from its aimless, fading whine. A flock of rooks whirred up out of a bare and solitary maple out in the field, and somewhere behind them the horned owl hooted again. From the bear there was no sound at all. Dushan scanned the edge of the forest with the binoculars; he tried the field as well, but search as he might, the bear was gone.

Slowly the tension loosened its grip, but this brought Dushan little relief, since it was replaced by a creeping feeling that as a hunter, which he considered himself to be, he had failed not once but twice. First, in planning the trip up to the bear's feeding site he had failed to put himself in the bear's place and foresee its reaction, even though he knew it was hungry and close by, and that the horse and donkey would represent a huge temptation. And then, firing this second shot had been not a well-considered act but rather one of complete panic when the bear had lunged right at him, out of the binoculars and straight into his brain, where it now remained, ready to spring again. A sense of uneasiness joined these gloomy thoughts as he also realized that people higher up were certainly going to expect a report. Because this bear was not listed in the records of any of the local districts, both encounters with it qualified as unusual incidents and would have to be described conscientiously, in minute detail. On top of all this Dushan was beginning to have doubts about the wisdom of having told the German gentleman about the bear before he had informed his superiors through official channels. He cursed his greedy desire for the beautiful products of the West, for it was this alone that had prompted him to write. Now he could only hope that the lapse wouldn't be noticed.

He felt thoroughly miserable. He lit another cigarette, but the casual observation that his hand had stopped trembling didn't cheer him; it simply reminded him of how frightened he had been when he'd lit the first one and hid it behind the pile of rocks where he was still standing. The thought sent a shiver running between his shoulder blades, and suddenly he longed for the safety of a shooting stand, and the certainty of regulations. Since they relieved him of all major decisions, it was hard for him to make minor ones, such as approaching the donkey carcass, but he forced himself to do it now, with the cocked rifle tucked under his left arm and pointed at the forest, his right index finger on the trigger. That alone was enough to make him break out in a cold sweat. And then to have to inspect the scene where his violation of the regulations had ended in defeat—this site of personal disaster! He leaned his rifle against the toppled cart and groped hastily for the gas lamp under the tarpaulin lying half on, half off the carcass. Since it appeared not to be damaged, he pumped up the pressure, struck a match, and lit it.

The flame flared up with a soft popping noise. The carcass had continued to swell. The mouth, now blue, flashed a row of long yellow teeth, the donkey grinning diabolically at Dushan's humiliation. In disgust he pulled the tarpaulin over its head and gave it a sharp kick. Then he heaved the cart onto the back end, so that the shafts stuck straight up in the air, and hung the lamp on one of them by his belt. Next he took off his jacket and sweater, laid them over a wheel with as much care as if he had been at home, and, clad only in his undershirt, lifted an armpit to his nose. He decided that the odor of sweat clinging to the shirt was strong enough for what he had in mind. Pulling it over his head, he knotted it around the other cart shaft at the same height as the lamp. This would let the night wind, now blowing gently toward the forest edge, carry the deceptive odor of Dushan's presence to the bear and keep it away from the carcass until morning. By sunrise Dushan planned to be back with the horse and two or three young men from the village and then finally to deliver the carcass to its legitimate place.

Once more he surveyed the theatrically illuminated scene, found everything in order, and, dressed again in his sweater and jacket, set out for home. Several times he glanced back, his rifle at the ready under his arm. But that he had put the safety on reflected a bit of returning optimism, a feeling that he would be able to handle the things he saw coming his way, unpleasant though they might be. To drive away the last remnants of his fear of the bear, he even whistled a little tune.

Joop was in the habit of taking work home in the evening when the atmosphere of the bank began to grate on him, and as he finished up the day's tasks he liked to have the television set on at the same time. This was prompted by a need he could never explain rationally to have some company, some life around him, after the stillness of a long day in his well-insulated office, although he rarely paid attention to what the voices that reached his ear were saying. Nor did he watch the screen as he sat hunched over his numbers and market analyses. It took something most unusual to shake his concentration on bank business—an interesting voice, an intelligent remark, a mysterious noise that advanced like a gust of wind and fluttered the curtain he had drawn around his awareness. And so, like someone getting up and going to the window to check on the weather when the curtain suddenly blows into the room, Joop at such moments would swivel his chair around and look at the set. Not for long, usually; after a short glance he would turn back to his papers. He moved in circles where television was regarded as the equivalent in cultural terms of an open shirt collar; Joop himself considered most programs to be cheap products aimed at the very bottom end of the market. And because Joop was also in the habit of asking the monetary worth of almost everything life had to offer, it was only logical for him to keep the set on until late at night when he was working at home; in addition to creating the illusion of his being a participant in life, it gave him the feeling of getting at least a little something in return for the monthly television tax he paid.

Joop particularly enjoyed this sort of whimsical bookkeeping, because he saw it as proof that his hunting companions were wrong when they claimed, as he knew they did, that he had no sense of humor. But his humor was of a kind that easily goes unnoticed at stag parties. In this regard he would never fit in; he considered getting a little blood on his shirt cuffs (something that can easily happen when you gut a deer, since *après*-kill etiquette forbids rolling up your sleeves) more pardonable than the verbal dirt that passed for humor among hunters when the hour got late.

On one such evening at home he was sitting and thinking, with the usual background noise, about how to answer a letter. The chairman of the board of his bank had asked whether he would like to act as a consultant to the World Bank and inspect a few development projects in Eastern Europe for which loans had been requested. His reverie was abruptly shattered by a deep, loud growl, and as he turned toward the screen, he found himself being stared at by an angry brown bear.

It was shown in close-up. Joop was familiar enough with popular literature on bears to realize at once that the face belonged to a grizzly. The size of the head suggested it, and so did the aggression expressed by its flattened ears and glittering eyes. Joop had read that white foam at the corners of a bear's open mouth is a sign of stress, and even before the camera pulled back he had guessed why this particular bear was so enraged. Sure enough, in the next shot you could see that it was standing in the middle of a garbage dump, that it was one of a dozen bears being crowded and harried by a group of tourists brandishing cameras. A ranger in a uniform that identified him as an employee of a U.S. national park was trying with emphatic gestures to herd back the all-too-careless sightseers. Then the scene shifted to show the bears rummaging pleasurably in more garbage, and the camera lingered just as pleasurably in close-ups of the bears' heads as one or another looked up from the nasty heap with its nose in a plastic bag or with a yogurt container stuck on its ear.

Joop's thoughts drifted away from these depressing pictures; for him as a hunter they seemed to confirm that a bullet at the end of a harsh life in the wild was a better fate for an animal than to live well-fed to old age amid the spiritual and material trash of civilization. He turned away from the documentary on what a naturalist like Konrad Lorenz would probably have called *the domestic pigification of the bear,* and went back to his chairman's letter. With half an ear he heard the commentator say that scientists were learning a great deal more about bears' behavior, the patterns of their comings and goings, their sleeping and waking. It was all made possible by new technology that used collars with mini-transmitters and even satellites. It must be a film from the sixties, thought Joop, who vaguely remembered reading something in a newspaper about garbage dumps having been closed in the American national parks where bears lived, with the aim of breaking off the close relationship that had developed between them and man. This had not changed his opinion on hunting, however, or on the questionable wisdom of allowing animal populations to multiply by forbidding it.

He now put the subject of bears out of his mind entirely and read on; the World Bank was interested in his participation, said the letter, since they had heard in New York about his trips to Eastern Europe, where he had twice gone hunting with the most influential government leader in the region. They were counting on his firsthand knowledge, not only of the country and its people but also of the current political situation, certainly the trickiest factor in deciding about the loans. With the nonchalance of a man who is used to seeing even facets of his private life become an object of interest to the media, Joop took it as a tribute to his professionalism that his passion for hunting was known in New York; he would have been the first to admit it was not a bad way to make contacts. He was all the more annoyed to find it referred to later in the same letter as a *hobby*. He despised this word in connection with hunting, or at least with the kind of hunting he did. But it stirred in him a rush of memories about the untouched wildernesses of Eastern Europe that became mingled with a sense of anticipation. On his way to the bathroom he stopped by the gun rack in the hall and ran his hand over the silky walnut stock of his best and largest-caliber rifle. Of course there would be business to deal with, too; it would take some doing to fit everything in.

Once again the high forest gave the bear shelter. He had left it before, but unwisely, since its green-tinged twilight softened the terrors of his exposed form. It had been unwise to leave the protection of the trees for open country, where he could be seen by eyes that measured his size not in awe but in trophy points, that assessed his age not to learn about his past life but to plan the timing of his violent death. Back here among the tall trees, among their waving shadows on the forest floor and the gray trunks of the beeches, he was merely one more moving shadow. Where the beeches were stopped short by outcrops of limestone, the hollows were still full of snow. It was melting, but only slowly, the water trickling away into crevices and sinkholes; in the forest a carpet of undergrowth was revealed, with last year's berries still hanging on it, preserved under the winter's snow. Laboriously the bear picked them over. The leaves he ate along with the fruit turned the white froth at the corners of his mouth to green.

It was the second shot that had made him foam at the mouth; first the odor of meat had made his mouth water and then the whine of the ricocheting bullet above his head had set his trembling jaws to working until the saliva was whipped to a lather. In this condition he had plunged on and on through the night and the spruce trees, across the level ground, running into the old road here, the new road there, and rebounding off both like a billiard ball. The night was almost over when he came to a halt at the entrance to an underpass, big enough to let a farmer's wagon through, under the highway he already knew. But the road held no fear for him anymore, since on the other side he could hear the familiar soughing of the wind that meant the upland forest and safety. This was his goal. The far end of the underpass opened onto a large field in which stood a small roofed frame of the kind the local farmers used for hanging up their corn. The frame was empty, but so many ears of corn had been left lying around it that the bear was able to still the worst of his hunger. Afterward he climbed up into the woods.

The next morning, after his first meal of berries, he set out to explore the area. He encountered neither a path nor any other sign of humans. At one point he came across a sinkhole and decided to investigate it further. Crossing a slope that led down to it, he found that the far side of the depression was overhung by a snow-covered rock so infiltrated with roots that it was hard to say whether the stone was holding the tree in place, or the tree the stone. For a long time he sniffed the floor and walls of this cavelike recess; they gave off a faint scent of bear, but one so old it gave no real cause for concern. Then he tested the direction of the wind and found it favorable; as it was blowing toward the entrance to the hollow, nothing could take him by surprise. Pushing out of the way rocks that had fallen from above, he turned in a small circle like a dog, lay down with a soft growl, jiggled around on his belly until he got comfortable, and fell asleep at once, his head on his paws. He slept for two days and two nights, waking only for brief intervals.

When at long last he emerged from the cave, he stood up on his hind legs, reaching his full height, as if he were stiff and needed to stretch. In fact he was testing the wind at the weatherward edge of the sinkhole. It had snowed again, and all the news, both good and bad, that he usually picked up from the currents of wind skimming the ground was buried under the snow. It was as if someone had aired out the forest and put clean sheets on it, but this was of course not the animal's image. The bear dropped onto all fours in ill humor; as his paws hit the ground he let out an evil-smelling belch. He had no need to be reminded of his hunger, however, for it went with him everywhere like an indwelling shadow within his huge frame, craving meat and fading only slightly in the bright spots of his few pitiful meals. He shook the snow out of his fur and left the hollow the same way he had entered it two days before, mounting the slope that led to the forest.

Under his feet he could feel that the snow was only a thin layer. When he lay down and rolled in it anyway, to clean his fur, old leaves stuck to him, and he knocked his shoulder against a large flat stone. He got up and turned the stone over. A few wood lice came to light; he licked them up. From under another large stone he got a tongueful of little yellow ants; still another produced a wrinkled earthworm, and a fourth a clammy blindworm. He rejected a toad he turned up among the dead leaves; he knew from experience that its leathery, wart-encrusted skin would have an ugly taste. Two snail shells he bit through were empty. He spat out the pieces and trotted on. A thick-trunked spruce, the only evergreen among a group of light-hungry beeches, proved to be the rear guard of a mixed forest that began farther up the mountain; its solitary position piqued his curiosity. He sniffed around its roots for a long time, and finally began to dig where he could discern a faint scent of fur. Soon he had uncovered a hibernating dormouse, so lethargic it passed from its small to its large death without noticing. While the bear could still feel the cold morsel inside him on its way to his stomach, he noticed a baby owl not far away that had fallen out of its nest and was flapping helplessly in the snow. Grunting to the rhythm of his bounding stride, he was on it in a flash. Its attempt to flee, flailing its wings in the snow on the way to nowhere, ended in the bear's mouth. He swallowed the screeching bird whole, with beak, claws, and feathers; there wasn't enough of it to bother with chewing.

All was still again. The bear urinated, as he had licked up a great deal of snow that morning. Under a few more stones he found three lifeless spiders and a small yellow scorpion, which he let go. With an air of boredom he swung his paws first to the right, then to the left, dusting the snow off a few bushy plants whose green leaf tips had stuck up out of the whiteness and revealed their presence. He ate a few berries off them. There weren't many, and soon he gave up altogether the laborious business of looking for such meager crumbs.

Darkness fell early up here on the mountain. The bear had felt secure in the recess of the sinkhole, and so he followed his own trail back. But when he reached the slope leading down to it, he found it already occupied. A powerful old female bear came toward him; at her flanks she had two very small cubs. She was on her way from her winter den, where she had given birth, to one of the nearby bait sites she knew from the year before. When it began to snow and night was falling, she returned to the sinkhole, a place that had served her as a retreat during the previous summer. She let out a menacing growl, and the bear stopped at the top of the slope, stunned into immobility; it was his first encounter with his own species since he had left this place many years before. Because he showed no signs of retreating, the mother bear came bounding up the slope at him. Her impact knocked him down; she stood over him and bit down roughly on his snout and lower jaw. It took a hard swipe of his paw against her neck for him to free himself, but she immediately came at him again, and this time they both rolled down the incline into the hollow in the rocks. They fought on with increasing vehemence, the male in amazement and rather cautiously, the female in a true fury, and the outcome would have been uncertain had the two cubs not misunderstood their elders' roughhousing as an invitation to join in the game. In high spirits they flung themselves into the air, whirled around, and fell back into the snow, coming closer each time— too close for the mother bear, who had once lost a cub to a hungry old male. She turned away from this one, whom she obviously suspected of having the same designs on her young, and butted and slapped them back into the cave.

The bear took advantage of the respite and was retreating up the slope and into the forest when he heard the mother bear coming after him. At the top of the hollow she stopped and yelped at him three times. It had begun to snow harder, and soon each lost both sight and scent of the other. He had dropped into a steady gait. He went up the mountain, climbing past the fat fir trees, spruces, beeches, and sycamores. The snow was making it hard for him to pick up scents, and the darkness made it hard to see. He had to prick up his ears and turn his head from side to side to catch the many sounds of this patch of old forest: the rushing in the treetops when a gust of wind came over the crest and bent them down toward the valley, the rasp of tree rubbing against tree, or the crack made by an entangled branch snapping back into place or breaking. Soon the bear's fur was so white that once, when he stopped for a long time to listen, a big owl mistook him for a snow-covered boulder. Thinking that the white shape would make a good perch for spying out prey on the ground, the owl headed in for a landing. When the bear tossed his head up with a growl and took a swipe at the bird, it was so close to him that the downdraft from its wings blew the loose flakes off his back.

He went on, feeling his way up the slope of the mountain. Only the high ground offered safety; that alone took him beyond the reach of human intrigues (and while a bear's brain could certainly not tell him this, the calm beating of his heart up here could, or a mouth now white with snow instead of foam). But this climb—to a height where no one would be left to take his size alone as a sign of ferocity—was also making him feel his age with every step: his stiffened joints, his shrunken tendons, a heart that beat faster not only from physical exertion but out of a new kind of timidity. Once, this tendency of his had expressed itself merely as a certain caution in interpreting the world, and had left his heart unaffected. But now, at the end of a life spent apart from his kind, it was driving him deeper and deeper into the indignities of old age. The once-powerful teeth had grown yellow and cracked, yet his usual prey—lice and spiders, earthworms and ants—was now so negligible that he didn't need teeth. He used his claws on helpless, newborn animals, not on the solid muscles of cow's neck or sheep's flank he used to have at least twice a year, before and after his winter sleep. His powerful roar had become a moaning in the rain; his pelt hung on him in folds and no longer kept him warm, and sleep overpowered him as easily as winter had the dormouse.

It was observing all this that led Dushan to report in a second letter to Joop that the new rogue bear was old and timid; he had been scared off without much trouble the night before, and it would be as easy to get him accustomed to a particular bait site if they could just keep him from attacking livestock in the meantime and satisfy his tremendous appetite without breaking the regulations. Dushan promised Joop he would take care of everything, make sure everything was OK; then the bear would have to go. Had Mr. Joop already applied for a license? And would he please be sure to tell absolutely no one about the source of his information?

On three of the six days Joop devoted to his consulting work for the World Bank, he attended meetings in Vienna, Bucharest, and Belgrade. The three days in between he spent "on site" (as his report would later stress), listening to various proposals. Some colleagues presented requests for financing the construction of a dam in a remote Alpine valley; several agrarian engineers explained their plans for transforming a region of small farms into a few large collectives; a group of government bureaucrats had ideas on developing tourism in the region between the Danube and Drava rivers; still others wanted to develop new industrial parks along the River Sava.

They had been astonished, Joop learned later, by the request he had submitted before his trip for experts to take part in the discussions and present the environmental issues raised by each project. As the officials racked their brains to guess the motive behind it, they suddenly recalled his interest in hunting. After that they had not only treated the request as perfectly normal, but fulfilled it as if it were a matter of course and used it to parade their own progressive attitudes on conservation of natural resources. Of course, they assured Joop before he could even raise the question himself, these new projects would have no adverse effect, or only very little, on either hunting or the regional environment; but naturally they had steps planned to compensate for even slight shifts in micro-ecosystems. His hosts uttered this last word in German, without bothering to translate it into their own language. Joop was surprised but didn't stop to ask himself how the term could have traveled east so quickly when it was just coming into vogue among West German environmentalists. At home his role was becoming increasingly one of placating environmentalist groups, but here, where the habitats of plants and animals were still largely intact, he felt as if he were carrying the proverbial coals to Newcastle. He was even more surprised, but pleasantly so, by the way the men with whom he had discussions seemed to equate the concerns of environmental protection and hunting. This was definitely a controversial subject at home, as he had gathered from a few outspoken attacks on hunting in the media. He rejected the possibility that his hosts were merely saying what they thought he wanted to hear. They seemed genuinely interested, and he recalled how on the drive from one potential investment site to another, one of his hosts had interrupted Joop's reading of proposal papers to point out a large herd of red deer, more than forty strong, roaming the grasslands in broad daylight without fear. There must be far more harmony between hunters and people interested in preserving nature in these Eastern countries, thought Joop. He was a firm believer that they should be compatible at home, too; his own hunting was based on that attitude, after all.

He was equally disinclined to see the exquisite dinners to which he was invited as any attempt on his hosts' part to influence his recommendation on their requested loans. Of course they did tend to take place at secluded hunting lodges, where over coffee someone always suggested that he stay on, or come back, for a bit of shooting, whatever he fancied, red or roe deer, wild boar or pheasant, duck or geese (or it might even be possible to arrange a bustard). But entertaining a person on a scale that he is used to, that is already his normal standard, couldn't be considered *bribery,* could it? My God, what a word! said Joop to himself, dumbfounded by his own thought.

The banquet rooms where they dined invariably had on one wall a framed photograph of the ruler of the country in which Joop happened to be at the moment. (When he noticed that he was avoiding the word *dictator* even in his own thoughts, he decided that this was only appropriate neutrality toward the politics of the bank's major customers, which were no concern of his. He had always taken this approach; anything else would be unprofessional.) In these photographs, the *gentlemen* (the word he settled on) were always dressed as sportsmen, to match the rustic atmosphere of the lodge, either alone or in a circle of the respectful, earnest-looking officials with mustaches who had acted as their procurers. At their feet—they were always in boots—lay the kill, a buck or a bear; none of them were ever depicted with anything smaller. They held their large-caliber rifles with mounted telescopic sights by the barrel, resting the stock on the dead animal's neck, but the triumphant victorious expression and jutting chin that should go with the pose were missing.

One evening Joop ventured a remark on this last point to one of the environmental experts in the group, a little professor whose corduroy trousers and sweater seemed overcasual even for a socialist dinner party. After a swift glance over his shoulder the environmentalist had replied with an inscrutable, melancholy smile that these men were enlightened democrats; you could tell by the fact that they didn't set a boot as well as a gun on their victim's neck. Joop had a feeling that as the representative of a neutral institution such as the World Bank he ought to take offense at this somehow, but he decided merely to object silently to the word *victim*, which he considered out of place when speaking of hunting. He said nothing aloud, and the little professor immediately moved on to a group of colleagues chatting nearby.

There were always antlers hanging on the lodge walls, but none ever matched the magnificence of the trophies in the rulers' photographs: those branches as thick as a man's arm, so many shimmering ivory points, the heavy pearling! The word *monstrosities* suddenly shot into Joop's head, and he realized in amazement that it expressed an inner revulsion, almost Freudian in its intensity, at what he was seeing. He was about to take refuge in his normal attitude—that such splendid heads merely reflected splendid standards of game preservation—when he noticed that the little professor had reappeared at his side. From a biological point of view, murmured the expert, these bulky excrescences were complete nonsense, and not at all adapted to life in the forest; they were only a nuisance to the stags themselves and of no interest at all to the females. Why people would hang these calcified swagger sticks on their walls was beyond him; it might be to venerate some sort of atheistic sacred cow, if that weren't a contradiction in itself. He did wonder, though, what would make an intelligent person, who otherwise thought strictly in terms of cost-effectiveness, pay up to thirty-five or forty thousand dollars to acquire a couple of pounds of old horns. The stags shed them every February of their lives, presumably with a feeling of relief, and the descendants of the hunters, once they were dead, would no doubt shrug their shoulders and put them out for the trash collectors.

Joop was once more spared the necessity of replying, since the little man disappeared again immediately. The professor ought to have stayed to observe the effect of his words, for Joop's face now reflected the confusion of his own feelings. He was wondering whether the professor's fiery speech had brought to a boil a muddy brew of doubts that had been simmering in his own mind for a long time about the sense of collecting trophies; it was as if the heretical word *monstrosities* had bubbled up from the bottom and splattered an object he had until then always held in veneration.

Prompted by a desire to think about something else, Joop turned to some of the other pictures on the walls, one of which showed some prominent sportsmen, including two German friends of his, with a bear they had killed. For a moment the photograph revived his flagging interest in going hunting. But at the same time another thought bubbled up from the doubts stewing in the depths of his mind: *You're just envious.* On the long list of game Joop had bagged, there was as yet no bear.

He burst the bubble with a yawn. But somehow he slept poorly that night, as the wind moaned in the treetops.

Joop had arranged for his company car, an expensive sedan, to be driven east for him. He himself had come by air and been ferried back and forth between the various capitals in the bank's small jet, but he would return in the car his chauffeur was now bringing. Except for Joop's guns and a few pieces of luggage in the trunk, the car was empty.

Whenever there was a chance he might be able to fit in some hunting, Joop always took three guns along on trips: The first was a double-barreled shotgun, made by Siace, with an exposed hammer and an automatic cocking mechanism; almost entirely handmade, it had an English-style stock of fine-grained walnut and delicate arabesque engraving on the receiver. The second was a Blaser bolt-action rifle, a 270 Winchester he used with 8.4 gram "Silvertip" bullets. The exquisite engravings on the side plates above the trigger guard had been made to order according to Joop's instructions and showed animal scenes: a pack of wild boar on one side and a herd of stags in the mountains on the other. The mount for the telescopic sight (made by Zeiss) was lavishly ornamented with an engraved oak-leaf pattern and a tasteful gold border that harmonized perfectly with the gold trigger and, as chance would have it, with Joop's gold-rimmed spectacles as well. The pistol grip had fine checkering to keep the marksman's sweaty hand from slipping, and a cap of heavy silver engraved with Joop's monogram. The pride of his collection, however, was his "bear slayer," a Heym over-and-under rifle. It had a box lock of the Anson and Deeley type and a sliding safety that enabled the marksman to fire quickly, something that in an emergency could mean the difference between life and death. The insurance company had set the value of all three weapons together at fifty thousand dollars.

When Joop went hunting, the guns traveled in their made-to-measure cases of moss-green sail-cloth and rode one above the other in mounts Joop had had constructed for the back wall of the trunk of his car, the lightweight shotgun on top, the heavy rifle on the bottom. The design of the car had also allowed him to remove a section of the floor of the trunk and insert a metal box resembling a safe into the opening; its lid was flush with the floor and covered with the same carpet material as the trunk, so that the whole construction was almost invisible when in place. If Joop had his guns along, this container held a day's supply or so of ammunition in various calibers. A few bags filled with hygroscopic material made sure Joop followed his own maxim, which he had had engraved on a brass plate and attached to the inside of the lid: KEEP YOUR POWDER DRY. Like the ammunition, the guns were relatively inconspicuous once in place, and someone glancing into the trunk might easily assume the cases held golf clubs, especially since the opulence of Joop's car suggested a natural kinship with such a sport.

Each of Joop's guns had a document for crossing frontiers, a kind of passport of its own, naming its make, type, and caliber, and of course the owner, as well as its identifying marks, such as hand-engraved hunting motifs in the style of the famous sporting-print maker Ridinger or the striking grain in the wood of a stock. In addition to space on the back for visas, each of these documents had attached a photograph of the weapon (embossed with an official seal), to permit identification by border guards even if there were communication problems. Joop hardly ever needed the documents,

however, since he also possessed certificates is-
sued—in the relevant languages—by the Eastern
European countries where he liked to hunt that
identified him *until further notice* as a guest of the
state whose luggage and sporting weapons should
be allowed to pass with as little inconvenience as
possible for their owner or, if applicable, his representative. For one of these countries the certificate
came from the office of the premier himself, whom
Joop knew rather well, and had been signed by him
personally, making it virtually the equivalent of a
diplomatic passport. "A gesture of comradeship
among hunters," the great man had said jovially as
he handed it over, with a slightly malicious stress
on *comrade*. Joop had let it pass, as he recalled,
with a faint smile. He preferred to recall the effect
this document produced at the frontier of the country in question. And this time, too, he could vividly
imagine how the border crossing would proceed,
even in his own absence: The guard steps up to the
window on the driver's side, which the chauffeur
has rolled down, and is handed the licenses for the
guns and the state document. He reads on, with
increasing attention, until finally he goes rigid with
astonishment; his eyes have fallen on the signature,
known to everyone in the country, of the man
whose picture is hanging over the captain's desk on
the wall of his guardroom. No thought now of
inspecting the firearms or the rest of the luggage;
clicking his heels smartly, the man salutes, a gesture of respect that is naturally not meant for the
chauffeur, just as it had not been meant for Joop on

the two or three occasions he had been in the car. No, *the guard is saluting the signature,* from which he will not take his eyes until his hand has left his cap brim.

That was certainly how it would go again, thought Joop as he lay in bed, his mind turning toward the private phase of his trip now that its official part was ending. He considered this little ceremony one of the nicer perks his very demanding job offered, and he had never said a word about it to friends and colleagues who also came to these East European countries to hunt. Like him, they came to hunt game that was declining in quality or all but ceasing to exist at home as the ravages of civilization encroached on or destroyed its environment. He never mentioned his own privileged status as a more or less official visitor, however; he would have considered it a breach of bank confidentiality, which in a certain sense it was, he felt. But on further consideration the thought seemed a bit too cynical, and thus not well suited to helping him fall asleep. Another of Joop's maxims required him to be absolutely honest with himself in his last thoughts at night and first ones in the morning; he considered it a kind of rudimentary, masculine prayer that revived his conscience after the daily battering it received at work. But today he was unable to think of anything more idealistic than bank confidentiality, and he fell asleep guilty of a venial sin.

When a bear comes back to a forest for the first time in the spring and the wind carries the news to the other animals, the atmosphere changes. The air grows heavy with the scent of fear given off by all those who regard him as their enemy, and he is the enemy of all who betray their presence by their urine, their droppings, or the shock waves of their throbbing blood—faint traces from mice and rabbits, powerful odors from deer and wild boar. More shock waves from their heads thrown up in fright, from their noses quivering to locate the bear, from the ears directed like sensitive antennae, from the tails waving in the air, and from the paws and claws dug so hard into the ground by quivering muscles prepared for flight that the uneasiness is communicated to the beetles and spiders, the snakes, frogs, and lizards. Then these stop, too, and—with feelers twitching, throats pulsing, tongues darting—test the air.

The agitation in the trees is of a different kind. It is the season of rising sap, of water mounting in columns no broader than a hair, tracing in countless forks and branchings the outline of every tree, like the blood vessels in a human body. As the wind stirs them, the trees look and sound as if they have put their heads together for a good gossip; the firs and spruces have needle-sharp tongues, and the maples and beeches pass along juicy whispers. In May, just about anything seems believable—and it is May now.

The snow that fell the night the bear came up the mountain hasn't lasted. And now here he is, surrounded by nature's great surge into life, turning over rocks again in search of the smallest prey. He knows the others are there, certainly; he can sense the large animals and the circle of fear all around him, but they are too fast for him. He is tired and weak from hunger. Soon there won't be much left under the stones, either. He knows he must move on. He steps up his pace from a walk to a trot and from a trot to a rolling gallop, without knowing where it will lead.

It turns out to be a large clearing, a place in the forest where a winter storm has swept through and uprooted the trees, leaving them lying helter-skelter in a tangle of trunks and branches. Over on the far side someone has already set to work cleaning up. Here and there lie untidy heaps of sawed and split logs, and in one spot someone has started to make a charcoal kiln. Whoever it is has already built the central chimney, which is a frame of tall stakes; later he will pile the wood around it, cover it with grass, light the fire in the middle, and turn the wood to charcoal. For now, however, the chimney is cold; the wood must dry before the kiln can be lit. There is a ladder leaning against the chimney, but there is no one on it. Not that the bear is expecting to see the charcoal maker there. He knows nothing about this or any other charcoal maker. He doesn't know what he is seeing, nor has he ever seen anything like it before.

The bear rises up onto his hind legs and rests his front paws on a tree trunk lying across several others at chest height. Hidden by the trees even when fully erect, he can survey the clearing, and he sees the charcoal maker. He doesn't know this is what he has seen, nor has he ever seen anything like him before. What the bear sees, with his weak eyes, is some kind of black animal moving slowly forward on all fours and stopping every so often, as if it were grazing. This is the charcoal maker, who is collecting in a tall basket pieces of wood for his kiln and pulling the basket along after him without getting up off his knees. Since the wind is blowing from behind the bear toward this strange animal, the bear can't get a whiff of any scent, no horn or hide, no droppings or urine. In the air there is nothing but the overpowering smell of freshly cut and bleeding wood.

The charcoal maker doesn't see him coming.

The bear moves around the edge of the clearing, hidden by the fallen trees. He takes care to avoid the twigs as he sets his paws down, so that they won't snap and give him away. When he has come halfway around, the wind is blowing from one side, and he stops, puzzled. He still can't make out what this creature is; neither his nose nor his eyes have recognized anything familiar. It continues grazing, black, its head down. The bear can't make anything of the basket or the split logs, either, and he can recognize a human being only by its odor and its upright walk: He perceives neither at the moment. And even if he could, he wouldn't want to know. Only three more bounds and he'll be on this animal, whatever it is, and even if there were any caution, any suspicion, left in him, it couldn't hold him back now; he has been without food for too long. He lunges forward.

The paw hits the charcoal maker on the shoulder and knocks him over. A short, slight man, he is thrown onto his back with such force that he keeps rolling and lands on his stomach. But as he spins he sees the bear standing over him, and the bear sees the man. Now the bear recognizes what the creature is, mostly by its shape as it lies with its legs straight. The charcoal maker has worked in these bear-infested woods for many years, usually alone, and although no one really knows what a hungry bear will do when it encounters a human being, the charcoal maker has heard that the best way to save himself from being eaten is to play dead. So he plays dead.

In fact it is unlikely that this would have done him any good; the bear is too ravenous for meat. What saves the charcoal maker is the smell of his skin and clothes. The smoke of all the kilns he has built over the years has turned both black; it has seeped into his pores, and there it stays, no matter how often he washes. And this acrid smell of smoke is similar to the smell of tar. It is not so long ago that the bear landed in the tar on the road; he still has traces of it on the soles of his feet. He pulls back, snorting with disgust. The charcoal maker is wise and brave enough not to move. After a while he risks a peek under one arm and sees the bear standing less than fifty paces away, at the edge of the forest. They watch each other for a long time, since a great deal is at stake for both. For both it is a matter of life and death, his own life for the man, the man's death for the bear.

The charcoal maker is a patient man. If he had ever been the kind to panic, his long life in the woods has trained him to act otherwise. And the bear is patient, waiting for a sign that will reveal to him the true nature of his prey, whether it is dead or alive, and what the horrible smell means that reminds him of the road and the sticky mass under his feet. The bear is also patient because if he gives up and goes away, he will have to start turning over stones again for prey he can swallow without using his teeth. The charcoal maker considers running over to the ladder leaning against the twelve-foot-tall chimney frame of the kiln he is building. But he rejects the idea, since the bear is too fast over a short distance for him to be able to make it; besides, the bear could climb the frame without much trouble. What is going through the bear's mind no man can say.

And suddenly it doesn't matter. The sound of men's voices can be heard in the forest behind the clearing where the charcoal maker is still playing dead. The voices are coming closer, and they belong to three woodcutters. Carrying chain saws, the men are on their way to the clearing to do some more cleaning up, and to saw some wood for the charcoal maker's kiln. The bear moves back under cover, behind the trees, and waits. He is not ready to give up this big prize just yet; with every yard he retreats the more its dreadful smell fades, and without the smell it immediately becomes more attractive again. The men reach the charcoal maker, who gets up, clutching his mauled shoulder, and quickly tells them what has happened. The three men switch on their power saws and march resolutely toward the edge of the forest where the bear was last seen, holding their wailing saws out in front of them like swords. When they arrive at the spot, the bear is gone. Although they exclaim over their disappointment, they are in fact relieved, and on the way back to the center of the clearing—where there is certainly no bear anymore—they keep their saws running just for good measure.

Two days later Dushan read all about it in the newspaper. The story told him where the rogue bear was, or at least where he should start looking for it. Then he would have to lure it out of the woods and down to the valley, to a bait station, where it could be killed for the general good of society, in full conformity with the regulations. Dushan just hoped the militia wouldn't be called out to hunt it down first.

At the time all this occurred Joop was still in the country. New York had requested an interview with the premier, and the State Chancellery had written to say that the great man would be most pleased to grant Joop an audience. It would take place at a secluded hunting lodge in the form of a "working dinner." When Joop asked his hosts about the place, they said it was in an area of lowland forest not far from where they were. They also told him that the premier was already there, stalking a rather special roebuck. All the members of the delegation now wore broad grins, which suggested to Joop that there was a racy secret involved they would be only too glad to tell him. And so he assumed an inquiring expression, more out of politeness than genuine curiosity, and learned that this particular buck had unusually magnificent antlers even for this part of the world; they might possibly set a record. The dictator (again, to use a term never mentioned) had been following their development for several years by means of photographs his staff was required to take. Joop thought to himself: *It's like a trophy display of a living animal!* The idea delighted him. He was not too fond of the German version, in which hunters hang all the trophies they have collected in one region and season on a tavern wall and ceremoniously admire one another's successes in clouds of rhetoric and cigar smoke, while a loudspeaker blares suitable music, usually excerpts from *Der Freischütz*. Joop hated opera, and in his opinion that kind of trophy show belonged in the same category.

Since his hosts' faces continued to wear suggestive smiles, Joop guessed that the sensational size of this buck's equipment was not limited to its antlers. And so it was: Speaking very freely (something Joop's hosts wished him to believe was typically allowed in their country), they told him that the story of this well-endowed animal and the premier's obsession with it was making the rounds among hunters all over the country, to general amusement. Apparently the great man carried photographs of his newfound passion in his wallet, where they replaced pictures of his wife. Her photographs had perhaps grown too bulky, people surmised, since over the years the lady had put on a bit of weight (not the expression they used). Joop forced a smile and walked away, thinking that the kind of trophy show put on at home might not be so bad after all. He had to dispatch a message to the State Chancellery that he would be happy to attend the dinner. The invitation filled him with a measure of pride, as he himself would have said had he been asked to describe his feelings at that moment: *"a measure,"* since his banker's caution reminded him that he should by no means take the honor of the meeting too personally, but *"pride"* all the same. After all, this would not be their first meeting; they were almost friends, and fellow hunters in any case.

The audience was not to take place until four days later, presumably because the premier was busy hunting his roebuck. Joop notified his office and decided to spend the intervening time on a small hunting trip of his own; his car and guns had arrived in the meantime. (The chauffeur had confirmed entirely Joop's vision of the border crossing.) He chose a game preserve that was not far away, known all over Europe for the size of its red deer. It wasn't the time of year to hunt stags, since their antlers were still growing and in velvet, but he wanted to see the area again, and it had good roebucks, too, on which the season was open.

Joop had yet another reason for picking this district. Not far from it lay a tract of land that had once been a large private estate, one he knew quite well. He knew it too well, in fact, to be able to suppress all the memories it called up now that he was closer to it than he had ever been on his recent visits to the country. It was the site of a love affair, and although the affair was finished, done with, Joop had never quite got over it. As so often in his life, he had created a certain external order to cover up an untidy jumble of inner feelings.

This old estate—a word that certainly no longer fit the political landscape of the country—had belonged to the family of his second wife. It was she who had been the great love of his life, although they had now been divorced for many years. They had not only spent their honeymoon there, but also visited it a number of times to go hunting; these were weeks devoted to a passion directed not so much at each other, Joop now believed, as at their common pursuit of the rich and varied local game. This passion had done more than bring them together; it had kept them together in an inexhaustible flow of talk about their cherished sport. Until it became evident that killing together was not a sufficient basis for a life together.

Mari was the youngest child of an old noble family of the Austro-Hungarian Empire, and the only survivor of it. Two world wars, she used to say in a tone of assumed indifference when the subject came up, had seen to it that the Czerkys and everything they owned had become history, except for her, a small town house in Vienna, and this estate. Until her marriage she had earned her living as the head of the foreign-language bureau of a United Nations agency in Vienna. Joop's visits to the town house had been few; he knew the estate better. He remembered it exactly: a round two-story tower with long one-story extensions on both sides. The two wings extended slightly forward in a shallow angle, so that the building as a whole resembled a pheasant about to take flight—at least it did in Mari's imagination. The impression was further strengthened by the red roof on the tower with two small round windows in it like eyes, and the pattern of red and green glazed roof tiles on the two wings. Inside the tower a baroque staircase of white stone led from the front hall to a gallery and an apartment on the upper floor that consisted of three small, interconnected rooms whose windows offered a lovely view of the Danube and the forests along its banks.

After the seizure of the property by the Communist régime, the wings of Mari's stone pheasant had been blocked off from the tower on both sides. Then the new owners (the state) knocked down most of the interior walls and replaced them with cast-iron columns that looked like streetlamps. All this gave the wings, which had once housed people and kitchens, the melancholy air of overgrown coach houses. The effect was fully intended, for from near and far they had brought together old hunting carriages that once belonged to the aristocracy and were now the property of The People. There were two- and four-wheeled vehicles among them, carriages for one or more horses, elegant conveyances and carts suitable for only the more rustic sorts of hunting. After cleaning and polishing they had been lined up in one of the wings, while the other was filled with coachmen's gear, harnesses, and lackeys' uniforms.

The motives behind this exhibition had never been clear to Joop. His first guess, then as now, would have been a desire on the part of the country's new rulers to demonstrate that they had banished the old ruling class for good; they had put the aristocrats' carriages on display, and the people, like the horses, were now freed from their oppressive yoke. On the other hand, Joop supposed, it might have been to preserve the local hunting traditions of a region so rich in game. After all, the sport had come to provide the country's new masters with as much pleasure as it had the old, and it provided them with Western currency as well when they hit on the idea of selling the more valuable animals for exorbitant fees. As always, thought Joop, exploitation of one group by another doesn't cease in a revolution; only the players change: In this case it had dropped one rung down the evolutionary ladder, and the newest class to be exploited was animals. Hunting has always been the great social leveler, Joop mused as the car continued on its journey into his past; it has a far greater effect on revolutionary zealots than do their principles, which they soon abandon anyway. Social upheavals just mean that a new set of people goes hunting.

Mari could no longer own the house, but with the aid of Western diplomats she knew both socially and professionally, she had won back the right to use the central tower. Joop had lent a helping hand, too, after he and Mari met in Austria at a shooting party where the guest list had been studded with the names of titled aristocrats and the newer barons of commerce. Even in those days Joop had considerable influence on bank policy with respect to Eastern Europe, whose governments were beginning to grow disenchanted with Moscow. Not everything red in the East was the glow of a new dawn (although not all that glittered in the West was gold, either). Ideological currencies were beginning to be traded, in fact, at fluctuating prices.

The people living near the old estate soon lost whatever interest they may have had in looking at symbols of a past régime. Their new rulers went hunting in automobiles; that was the only difference the museum conveyed to the populace, and before long the place was as quiet as before. The interior of the tower, including the furniture, was left untouched; there were plans to house a museum caretaker there, but these were dropped even before Joop and Mari's first visit.

The car was now close to the famous game preserve, and Joop thought that Mari's stone pheasant couldn't be far off. But when he saw the turnoff ahead he lapsed into a state close to panic. What was he doing there? Trying to contact Mari's spirit? he asked himself ironically. She had long since remarried—an American diplomat—and moved to California. (At the time, he had soothed his wounded ego with the thought that she had married this man only to get to America; she was tired of Europe, tired of feeling like a refugee, of having to visit her childhood home as a paying tourist. And she was tired of hunting.) So what in the world was he doing there? Something else must be drawing him back to the house.

Paralyzed by these warring impulses, Joop let the chauffeur drive past the turnoff. Only then did he pull himself together and reach a decision. Feeling suddenly tired, listless, and old beyond his years, he asked the driver to turn around and go back to the side road. Even without slowing down, he had recognized it from the shape of a certain clump of trees. How little trees alter with the years, he thought morosely.

Three days after the attack on the charcoal maker, a commission of high officials from the Forestry and Wildlife bureaus found fresh, light-colored bear scat in the clearing, and trees scarred with claw slashes so deep and so high that only a bear could have made them. The charcoal maker and the woodcutters were refusing to continue their work under the bear's very nose, as they put it. The commission debated calling out the militia to attend to the bear. At this critical moment, Dushan, who was present in his role as the district game warden, made a suggestion:

He would like the comrade officials to keep in mind the amount of The People's money this bear represented—as well as its hunger, which, although it was the cause of all the trouble, might still be put to good use. If the militia simply killed the bear, it would be gone, but so would all the money those rich Germans threw around so casually for a chance to go bear hunting. Of course he knew what the comrades were thinking: the regulations! The regulations prescribed that a registered, fee-paying hunter could shoot at a bear only from a stand erected for the purpose. And here in the clearing there was no such stand, that was true. But nothing in the regulations said they couldn't build one. If the bear won't come to the stand, then the stand must come to the bear, he said slyly, laughing to keep up his courage. There was certainly enough wood lying around to build a blind, and the fallen trees had to be cleared away in any case—in the interest of good forest management, he added quickly for the ears of the forestry officials present. Dushan knew them well, and thought of them as "advocates of poplar government." With this pun, which said everything negative and therefore accurate about these forestry people, whose heads were full of nothing but lumber and money and management, never what was good for the wild-life, who yammered about every tree on which a bear sharpened its claws, every sapling gnawed by a deer, and mourned every scraggly little bent pine on which a buck polished its antlers—with this pun on *popular* Dushan had once described the state forestry bureaucrats to Joop, because of their eternal preoccupation with planting poplar trees. Poplars grow fast, poplars bring in money, and poplars stand obediently in rank and file.

Dushan was wise enough to keep his thoughts to himself here, however, and said aloud merely that the place had to be cleared, obviously, so that all this good wood wouldn't go to waste. And his idea would let them kill two birds with one stone, so to speak, for if they first made a corridor to give the hunter a clear shot, they could use it later for bringing in logging trucks. The bear would amble in at its leisure to take the bait, but it would never depart again, since if there was one thing these Germans knew more about than making money, it was shooting. They would just have to come up with a hunter quickly. The Tourist Bureau in the provincial capital had long waiting lists of such people, who would drop everything at home on a moment's notice when the opportunity of a large bear beckoned.

And now about this particular bear. They knew it was still in the vicinity. And to make sure it stayed, Dushan explained, he would feed it, bring it to heel with meat, but with small portions only, to keep its hunger alive. At first, for as long as people had to be there to clear the corridor and build the shooting stand, he would set the bait out far from the clearing but not too far, and gradually the bait would hang closer and closer. He would nail it to trees, so that the foxes couldn't get at it. That way they could accustom the bear to the clearing, and the bear would make the connection in its mind with regular meals. They could carry on in this manner for four or five days, six if necessary, and that should be long enough to locate a paying hunter. He knew of one, in fact, if contrary to expectation such a person should prove hard to find, a German banker whom he had already taken out deer hunting, and who had mentioned at the time that he was interested in bears. At this point in his account Dushan shot his audience a quick glance out of the corner of his eye. But none of the comrades objected, and the looks they were exchanging seemed to say: Well, what do you know? This Dushan has a head on his shoulders!

Dushan concluded his speech: Once everything was prepared and the foreign hunter had arrived, he would serve up a whole horse in the dark hours before dawn and then wait in the stand with the guest, according to regulations. As soon as the light was good enough for a shot: *Bang!* The gentleman would have his bearskin and the government would have the money. What did the comrades say to that?

Before they could answer, Dushan hastily added one point. One of them would have to come along on the night of nights—armed, of course—wait until Dushan and the guest were up on the stand, and then leave. Why? Well, while the bear wasn't stupid, it still couldn't count to three. Until that night it would always have seen just one person coming and going with the meat. If it saw one man going away on that night, too, then in its greed to get at the food, the bear would forget the other two and believe it was alone with the bait.

The officials walked away from Dushan, the charcoal maker, and the woodcutters to deliberate, and stood whispering among themselves. Dushan was so certain they would approve his scheme that he quietly tucked a copy of the plans for a shooting stand into one of the woodcutters' hands. Like everything else in the country, these blinds were constructed according to government norms; local hunters referred to them contemptuously as shooting galleries for bears. Then Dushan showed the others the spot where he wanted the stand erected, as well as the length, breadth, and direction of the corridor. At this point the commission returned. They agreed to do everything just as Dushan had proposed. They would ask the Tourist Bureau to find a suitable hunter and take steps to have the other matters approved, such as the supply of stockyard refuse and permission for the comrade forest workers to start building the stand and clearing the corridor. Dushan saluted. And what about the third man, the one needed to deceive the bear? The leader surveyed the members of his delegation, who were all looking silently at the ground and shaking their heads. It was decided that they would send Dushan the game warden of the neighboring district.

And finally they put the big question to Dushan: Could he tell them—from his experience and because apart from the charcoal maker he was the only person to have seen this bear in the flesh—how high they ought to set the hunting fee? The amount would have to be mentioned in the offer to the hunter. Dushan didn't bother to reckon in the local currency; that sum, he thought, would be even more fearsome than the bear. He answered unhesitatingly, since the hope of all hunting guides for a tip to match the fee had prompted him already to give considerable thought to the matter: Thirty-five thousand dollars. With the exception of the charcoal maker, all of them had some idea of what that meant, since hunting fees were routinely calculated in Western currency. If, as would have been quite natural, the comrades made any comparisons between such a sum of money and their own annual salaries, they didn't show it. Instead they made haste to leave the clearing, for it was growing dark, their official cars were parked some distance away, and the forest through which they would have to go to reach them harbored a large and hungry bear. Dushan took up the rear guard, since he was the only one with a gun. He was thinking about how to get word to the German gentleman, to whom he had already written twice, about the new urgency.

The bear had in fact remained in the vicinity of the clearing. In a particularly damp and open patch of forest, he had found a large field of hogweed, whose luxuriant leaves grew from meaty underground tubers. That had been three days before. Since then, the patch had come to resemble a plowed field, so thoroughly had the bear dug up the soil and eaten the roots, one by one. This was the source of the light color and loose consistency of the scat he had deposited on his forays into the storm clearing, to which he had been driven by curiosity. The trees felled by the wind offered so much protection that he felt safe there even in the daytime. He slept, however, under an uprooted spruce tree that had escaped the notice of the foresters because it lay far from the clearing and the logging trails. The bear had dug under the plate of roots that had been torn out of the ground until there was a hole large enough for him to fit into. The mat of roots and soil offered shelter but was porous enough to let in scents from all directions.

He had slept through the committee meeting. Or rather, to put it more kindly, the clearing was too remote from his lair for his senses to inform him about what was going on there. But on the fourth morning after his attack on the charcoal maker, the wind bore a scent up the mountain that he knew only too well—a mixture of horse, man, carrion, and smoke.

The bear's nose hadn't deceived him: Dushan had begun carrying out the plan he had described the day before, and was on his way up to the storm clearing from the plain below. He was leading a horse again, which was loaded this time with two baskets; the terrain here was too rough for a cart. In the baskets lay four large chunks of donkey meat that had been delivered to Dushan's cottage long before dawn. He was smoking a cigarette as he walked. The path he was following went up to the elevation of the clearing but passed far to the west of it. On the day following the bear's attack on the charcoal maker, Dushan had inspected the clearing and found some faint tracks leading west, toward the area of the forest where he was now headed. The trail had soon disappeared, since the mossy ground was too springy to retain good impressions. And so it happened that without being aware of it, Dushan came much closer to the bear than he intended to, close enough for the bear to sniff his scent.

The bear didn't stir from his shelter, not even when he could hear the sound of the horse's hooves. The particular mixture of odors had taught him a lesson about dealing with man. Since the horse was walking with the wind at its back, it got no scent of the bear ahead, and so this trip proceeded uneventfully. Too far away for the bear's weak eyes but close enough for its nose to register, Dushan pulled the horse up against a tree, removed the basket on the near side, and placed his left leg into the stirrup to lift himself to where he could kneel in the saddle on the other leg. Giving the horse a friendly order not even to think of moving, which it obeyed, Dushan levered a piece of meat out of the remaining basket. He had already pierced it with a long carpenter's nail. With the meat held in his left hand securely against the tree, he pulled a hammer out of the shaft of his right boot and pounded the bait in firmly. He then repeated the procedure three times, at intervals of several hundred yards. The bear withdrew farther into its hole at each blow of the hammer. If anyone had run a line along the four trees now hung with bait up out of the foxes' reach, it would have exposed what the profusion of trees concealed: The trail of the bait led toward the clearing. Dushan was a master of his trade, which was to lure a bear where he wanted to have it.

He left the spot without lingering. If he added together the bear's hunger and the meat, he came up not with two, but with three reasons for his haste. It was altogether possible, he thought, that if the bear was nearby and made reckless by the odor of meat, it might want to make its first large meal of Dushan or his poor horse. And so he settled back into the saddle behind the baskets and spurred the horse toward the valley. He turned again and again to check each direction, to the left and right and behind him, his rifle at the ready, but all was still.

By the time Dushan had begun whistling a tune, however, far from the baited trees now and approaching the plain, the bear was ripping the first donkey haunch from its nail. He fell upon it with a bestial appetite that had already begun to corrupt his innermost nature, that would make tolerable the all but overpowering scent of men and their tools, and even the noise of their distant power saws in the clearing. Grunting and smacking his lips, his maw dripping with saliva, the whites of his eyes showing in his greed, he sank his teeth into the all too convenient prey. They had succeeded. *They had turned him into a vicious swine.* He didn't realize it, but he had become and would remain one. They had transformed him into a dancing bear now; the nose ring of their cunning held him fast, as it did the other bears in the region. His hide was nothing but a bagful of money.

Like a dream receding into deeper sleep, in Joop's memory the antlers in Mari's tower had retreated into the walls until they seemed only a faded pattern, like wallpaper, black and brown and ivory on a chalk-white ground. He remembered that there were hundreds and hundreds of them; they started at the foot of the baroque staircase and rose at the same angle as its stone handrail, climbing to the tower's second story and almost reaching its high ceilings. They ran from eye level up to the moldings in the gallery and the upper rooms; they were everywhere, framing the doors and the windows overlooking the Danube, too, at least twenty rows of them, one above the other. It was the family trophy collection, the haul of three generations of Czerkys. There were deer heads on all sides, with antlers in every possible state and shape: huge, stunted, straight, twisted, many-pointed and simple spikes, in shades ranging from off-white to black. Perfect specimens hung next to deformed and cancerous-looking wig-heads; tobacco-brown trophies with beautifully pearled coronets had sickly white buttons as neighbors. He recalled several heads swathed in mummified velvet, and two that even sported the rusty barbed wire in which their owners had once become entangled. Many had no mounting besides the tops of their own bleached skulls, while others sat on green-and-gold-painted plaques with hand-carved borders of oak leaves. Each bore the date and place of the kill, inscribed in india ink on the brow of the skull or painted on the wood.

Joop was greeted by the museum caretaker, a middle-aged woman on whom the passing years seemed to have weighed heavily, pressing her down and outward to a matronly girth everywhere: not only in the face under the black wool babushka, but also in the breasts under the black cotton blouse and on the hips under the black apron over the ankle-length black skirt over the black shoes and stockings. As Joop was getting out of the car, she emerged from the tower round and full like an eclipsed woman in the moon whose customary white is only a memory. *White* would have been the first word to come to mind if Joop had ever tried to recall her; in the old days, when she came to clean and take care of the house for Mari, she had worn white linen blouses that revealed a great

deal of fair skin. Now she was crossing the court-
yard like some darkened spheroid and trying, to his
embarrassment, to kiss his hand as she bobbed an
awkward curtsy. In contrast to Joop, she had recognized a face from the past without a second's
hesitation. She had heard about the divorce long
before, but now, overcome by memories of Mari,
she began to weep softly as she led him into the
tower. In a corner of the front hall stood a little
table with tickets for the carriage museum on it,
and her knitting; she was making something out of
black yarn. He was welcome to go upstairs, she
said, pointing, but unfortunately nothing was prepared. But if he wished . . . No, Joop wanted
nothing of the kind. He had no desire to stay and
said he would only look around for a bit, an hour
or two at the most.

Joop started up the staircase, which cut through
the forest of antlers like a ski trail on a mountain,
and paused in amazement, as if he were seeing it all
for the first time. Most eye-catching was a group of
magnificent stag heads. He didn't need to count
them. There were twelve of them, hanging just
where they always had. He had studied them,
knew their burnished points by heart, in fact, as
they had been thorns in his flesh from the beginning. He had felt stabs of envy every time he went
by. Each of these record-setting trophies hung in
the center of an empty circular space, as if the
smaller antlers were keeping a respectful distance.
The radius of the circle was determined by the span
between the stag's antlers. For a fraction of a sec-

ond Joop had a clear vision of himself during the last twenty years as just such a royal stag, before whom the others retreated or made subtle gestures of submission. As they fell back, however, they kept their eyes on him, looking up and studying him carefully from below, whetting their envy on him, the keen edge of their own ambition. As soon as the image occurred to him, it seemed too arrogant, so he substituted a harmless one: He tried comparing the antlers to trees. Projecting from their circles of empty wall, they reminded him of the solitary giants of the forest, who had their own way of keeping rivals at a distance: the long shadows cast by their branching tops.

The open door let in the warmth of the sun and a light breeze that flowed toward the ceiling, fluttering the cobwebs in the forks of the topmost antlers. Otherwise nothing stirred in them at all. The desiccated victims hanging there—flies, now sucked dry, whose mimicry of wasps had been to no avail, powdery moths who had thrown no dust in the spiders' eyes, butterflies whose beauty had left them cold—all held answers to the riddles of lives annihilated long ago (and the trophies on the tower walls even more so). But no one was asking questions. No one was interested in this ossified orgy of thwarted lives. The flesh had been eaten, the blood drunk, the bones picked clean and meticulously sorted.

Joop had arrived hoping to snare some inspiration for the hunting he had planned, but in Mari's stone pheasant there was nothing to capture but dust.

And new humiliation. Two of the three rooms on the upper floor of the tower had been used as bedrooms; now Joop entered the third, which had a fireplace and had served as their living room. The window was dirty and appeared to be stuck, so he had to endure the musty odor of unaired curtains and cushions. It would provide him with a reason for a swift departure, since he had immediately begun to regret having come at all. He had never forgotten the six chamois heads over the mantelpiece, much less the story behind them. The horns were mounted on ebony plaques; below the skulls, small silver inscription plates revealed that they were of relatively recent vintage. The inscriptions stated that they had all been killed in the same place and on the same day, three by Joop and the other three by Mari. In actual fact, all six belonged to Mari, and he burned with shame again at the memory.

He had never been a particularly good shot, while Mari's skill was almost incredible. Her aim was so accurate that she could afford to indulge a whim for which she became notorious. When she went hunting, she took only as many cartridges with her as the number of animals she had decided to kill, or the number to which she was entitled as an invited guest. It was the arrogant gesture of a hereditary aristocrat in a country that had declared itself a republic, where hereditary titles had been abolished and arrogance was tolerated only from bureaucrats and headwaiters. Laughing and flashing her white teeth, Mari flaunted her skill and became the talk of Viennese society. But no one could ever say they had seen her miss. Even in situations where other people would lie on the ground and steady the barrel of their gun on a rucksack, she would remain standing, balancing her gun on nothing more solid than her alpenstock. She adamantly refused ever to shoot from a stand; she hated to wait for anyone, and would make no exception for a stag. She despised even more the custom of shooting from a sitting position. If you were going to kill an animal, she said, at least you ought to have the decency to do it standing up.

Before the chamois hunt on that occasion she had told him they were each allowed three kills and that, as usual, she was taking three cartridges along. She and Joop took up the places their host had assigned them, and when the chamois appeared, fleeing before the beaters, she aimed and fired three times. The animals were bunched in a large herd, with not much space between them, but the three she chose all fell dead in their tracks. On the second beat it was Joop's turn. He aimed at a buck and missed, even though he was lying down and using his rucksack as a prop. Instead of a clean shot, he had blown off one of the animal's front legs. An instant later a shot was fired from behind him that cleanly killed the mutilated creature. When Joop looked around, Mari was still in the stance from which she had fired, her pelvis thrust forward and her upper body knocked back by the recoil of the gun. She blushed as she smiled down at him over the barrel and apologized for interfering. *Sorry,* she said, uncertain how he would take it, *but I thought that would make us look bad*. She had meant the horrible sight of the wounded buck, which had been catapulted head over heels and was attempting to flee on three legs.

In his amazement, Joop could think of only one thing: that Mari must have brought extra cartridges along. That was something she had never done before; her reputation as a crack shot depended on it. Then he began to feel deeply affronted. *She did it because she expected me to miss*, he thought. The goddess of the chase helping out a mere mortal. It was the foresight alone that wounded him—although he couldn't know what lay behind it. It could have been prompted by a wish, not fully conscious, to outdo the great Joop in at least one thing he cared about, since he was superior to her in everything else—more experienced, more sophisticated, richer. He accepted the coup de grace.

Unnerved now, he fired off two more bad shots. One pierced a lung and sent blood pouring out of the chamois's mouth, while the other hit the animal's backbone, leaving it paralyzed. Three times Mari made up for his shortcomings and dispatched the struggling creatures. After three such misses there was no more need to apologize.

By the end of the day someone had started a rumor that Mari Czerky (as she was still known to these people even after her marriage) had fired six times but made only three kills. When she heard it, she reacted with a laugh that neither confirmed nor denied it, and since there were no witnesses, her reputation suffered virtually no damage. And when the engraver came around to all the members of the shooting party, busily collecting orders for inscriptions and plaques, she ordered six in a voice loud enough for everyone to hear—three in her own name and three in Joop's. He accepted it without protest.

Before leaving the tower he glanced into Mari's bedroom. The heavy gilded frame above her narrow, virginal bed still held the same mirror of dimmed and discolored glass. In the old days, when they spent their summer vacations here, her reflection in it had reminded him of a painting cracked and faded with age. She often lay there, wearing very little in the hot weather, usually on her youthfully flat stomach. She was in her mid-thirties then, and childless; under the thin raw silk, so cool to the touch, her flesh was still smooth and firm. Her skin was white except for one violet-colored bruise just under her right collarbone; it never disappeared entirely during the hunting season and came from the kick of her hefty weapons.

It pleased her that he liked to kiss this particular spot. She called it "worshiping Diana," and she meant it in earnest. Her solemnity always frightened him, since it seemed to suggest that his main role in her eyes was as high priest of her own cult. Her face, with its naturally red lips, mobile nostrils, and gray eyes above prominent Slavic cheekbones, was tanned, like her hands and arms, from all the time she spent outdoors. Often she lay on her bed propped up on her elbows reading, usually a volume of Trakl. She liked the Austrian poet's intoxication with words, his overheated intensity that made her think of a rutting stag, although she sometimes quoted him in a mocking tone: *The dying hart so gently bleeds / And ravens splash in bloody gutters.* Or she would recite the opening lines of the "Grodek" poem, that spoke to her of the sad fate of her family after two world wars: *The autumn woods are loud tonight / With armies' deadly fire across the lakes / And golden plains. The sun rolls on above, / but darker now.* At times her voice would break and her eyes fill with tears. Then she would add one more line, like a terrible echo of the others: *All roads lead to the blackness of decay.*

Often as she lay on her bed reading she would run her sinewy hands, so skilled at bringing death, along the downy back of her neck and through her short black hair. In revenge for her remark about worshiping Diana, Joop called the picture of her reflected in the gold-framed mirror at such moments "Closed Season on Diana." Irony and admiration lay behind it, but also resignation and a presentiment of the parting of their ways.

He had seen her reflection as a portrait and given it that title one hot afternoon in June. He had been out deer hunting, with one successful kill that day, and came to her room with his shotgun dangling open over one shoulder and the smell of blood on his shirt and hands. He knocked at the door (they were still very considerate of each other's privacy even after several years of marriage) and found her with her back to him, sitting naked on the bed and looking at herself in the mirror. Any success? she asked, continuing to admire herself. He could see no trace of embarrassment in her eyes as he bent down to answer and held his head next to hers. Together they studied her reflection. She followed his gaze with amusement, laughing softly as it slipped from breasts to belly and down to her pubic hair. Feeling caught in the act of lustfulness, Joop quickly looked up. Their eyes met in the mirror, his glittering with desire, Mari's darting back and forth between them both, as if searching for some reflection in her own face of what she saw in his. As he stood and stared, hoping vainly for a flicker of response, his eyes shifted their focus and he saw a horrifying sight—the image now framed in gold and looking down at them from the wall was an exact recreation of the pose in a famous painting (it hung in the Prado, but the artist's name escaped him at this painful moment of self-exposure in another's eyes): "An Old Man Bending Lecherously Over a Naked Young Woman." The edges were blurred; the woman's pale body almost filled the frame. The thought flashed through his mind: Centuries of abuse have worn away the paint; male eyes and their carnal lusts have left it leached and scarred. This vision lasted only seconds; as he looked at the man's head again he recognized himself in a hot wave of shame, and his eyes refocused. He straightened up and in an instant had regained his self-possession, was once more the successful banker from head to toe.

And Mari? To him it seemed as if she were turning away in disgust from something filthy as she flung herself around, pressing her knees together tightly. Or was it not that at all? Was he only imagining that she felt disgusted because *he* felt dirty? Could it be that Mari was simply disappointed by his timidity, by his renewed failure at a critical moment—the moment not of death, as on that chamois hunt, but of the essence of life itself? (Joop groped for a keyword to sum up the whole painful business, so that he could file it away in his memory and retrieve it later in similarly delicate situations; his brain was functioning that efficiently again. And the first phrase to occur to him was *coitus interruptus mentalis*. But then he had rejected it as too cynical, too flat. In general he had noticed, with growing concern, that his innermost core was being invaded by cold terms from the computer world like *keyword, file,* and *retrieve;* it was as if his private nature were being eaten up by a dangerous virus that infected his feelings and turned his thoughts shallow.)

Whatever she was feeling, Mari swiftly covered herself up to her chin with a sheet and then began to quote more Trakl (at least he assumed it was Trakl; it was definitely ruttish). She recited the lines as if she had just been given a cue, as if the whole scene had been rehearsed and not experienced for the first time a moment before, and once again she had a glint of mockery in her eye: *And sometimes lustful glances meet / When breezes blow the barnyard through the parlor. . . .* So she had wanted to kill again after all, if only his desire for her! It had been enough for her that he smelled of blood and had given the picture she made on the bed a name. "Closed Season on Diana."

Mari had in fact been pleased with the name, as she had been with his "worshiping Diana," since with both he seemed to be saying that he understood her innermost being. When they were hunting, she would have to refuse herself to him. In the heat of this landscape and of the blood, two kinds of passion were one too many, not in a physical sense, but spiritually. One owed the animals a little decency. While other hunters fasted to lose their inconvenient extra pounds, Mari abstained to lose the sense of guilt she felt when she killed. She was sincere in feeling what Ortega called "a bitter taste in the mouth at the sight of beautiful animals killed," words that to most hunters were merely a rhetorical flourish at their banquets, chalk in the throats of wolves. When she laughed after shooting the chamois, she was expressing pleasure at the perfection of her skill, and if it was immoral, it was also divine: Diana reborn.

Now her chaste bed was draped with a white sheet, and the mirror empty. He would not hunt with her again. He went back to the living room and took down the three chamois heads with Mari's name engraved on their plaques. He left the heads labeled as his in place. On his way out of the tower he asked the caretaker for permission to take the trophies with him. Since she thought they were his own property, the woman feared no difficulties, and when she saw Mari's name on the plaques, she was convinced she understood his feelings. But she understood nothing; how could she, when Joop didn't understand himself? He could not have explained why he was taking the heads or what he would do with them. He hated the thought of hunting trophies on his walls at home, and it would be completely inappropriate to hang them at the bank. His colleagues would never let him hear the end of it.

Joop climbed wearily into the car and told his chauffeur to drive on to their final destination, the game preserve famous for its stags. Without turning around he raised a hand in a gesture of farewell the woman would be able to see through the rear window. He had not had the strength to utter all the polite words called for upon his departure from the tower, which he knew he would never see again. For him, Mari's pheasant had just fallen dead at his feet, pierced by a volley of bleak memories. He wished he were back on foot in the rain again, as he had been two weeks before, after recalling how he had made a fool of himself in front of an employee over the portrait of Diana. No one would be able to see the tears in his eyes then. He repeated the word: *Fool.*

The bear's journey from his temporary den under the fallen spruce tree to the meat was growing longer day by day, since each time the bait lay a little closer to the clearing. Every evening in the last light he caught the scent of the man who left it. Now he found the meat either on the ground or on a stump, and no longer nailed to a tree.

It wasn't necessary anymore. Each of them knew what he needed to know for his own safety about the other: The bear knew that the meat arrived in the evening and that the man who brought it went away again; and Dushan knew that the bear was taking the bait and would follow it from place to place just as he wished. He also knew that no fox would even think of going near the bait, since for all the other animals the forest south of the charcoal maker's clearing simply reeked of bear.

Dushan had also stopped taking the horse with him. After the first serving of donkey meat, which had been generously calculated, he had begun reducing the portions; the idea was to keep the bear manipulable by taking the edge off its appetite but not satisfying it. To find its dinner each evening, the bear had only to use its nose and follow the trail Dushan made by packing the day's portion of meat in his rucksack and dragging it along the ground from yesterday's bait site to the new one. It might be a neck of beef or donkey shoulder; another time it would be a leg of mutton. The bottom of the rucksack was encrusted with dried blood and so permeated with the odor of carrion that for a bear's nose it was equivalent to a brightly lighted highway. And in this case it could also be depended on to lead the bear to its goal.

Within the space of only five days the bear had grown so used to the new routine that when Dushan arrived, the animal had long since left its cave under the toppled spruce tree and was waiting near the previous day's bait site to follow Dushan to the next one. The bear hid each time in a long strip of forest that had been thickly replanted by the foresters ten or twelve years before, after a bad windstorm had brought down all the old trees. Dushan now drew the animal along this swath of forest toward the new storm clearing as surely as if he had a ring through the bear's nose. Dushan had lost his fear, even though he strongly suspected that the bear was lurking in the dense growth and waiting for him each evening when he arrived. He had set the bear firmly on the path of habit, where he kept the other bears under his supervision. And the bears of the region who were not under Dushan's supervision (he had heard they existed) fared no differently.

These other bears, it was said, were being raised directly by bureaucrats from the Wildlife Bureau for the great man in the capital. And *raised* was the right word for it, according to the stories making the rounds. In the villages at the edge of the great forests they were saying that their leader was obsessed with killing a bear that, once flayed, would surpass all other bears of Eastern Europe in the size, thickness, and splendor of its skin. He wanted to shoot the bear of all bears, one that would be his equal in power and authority, more his equal than the three or four other leaders of the East with whom he exchanged kisses before the television cameras and who hunted bears in their own countries, who even played host to one another for bear hunts, but who—he had solemnly sworn—would never kill a bear like the one he would kill in his own land someday.

And so the bureaucrats had to feed the bears for their leader, giving them meat to make them grow and corn to make their fur thick and shiny, as if the bureaucrats were raising dogs. In the hope that at least one of these bears would turn out to be a prize specimen, they served the animals meals that some of the peasants in this poverty-stricken area would have been happy to share, no doubt, if the food had only been cooked. They even thought of worm pills, mixing them in the bears' rations just as they had seen done on great estates in the West where industrialists and aristocrats bred their stags. Here, however, every ounce of every bear belonged to the great man in the capital.

When Dushan thought about these rumors after one of his trips to the bait site, he was inclined to believe they were true. The hope began to stir in him that this bear, his bear, just might be the special one. Its height was right, and so was the span of its limbs, although the quality of its fur might well be a problem. Dushan had noticed this, through the binoculars his German hunter had given him, the very first time he had encountered this bear among the willows in the valley. The mere thought of a record-setting bear made his heart beat faster. He would present his idea cautiously to the commission in whose hands the bear's fate now lay.

Now that Joop had summoned the spirits of environmentalism, he was finding he could not get rid of them. On his arrival at the hunting lodge where he was to meet the leader, they came out to greet him, four of them altogether, with the little professor in the lead, the one who had prophesied that the final destination of all antler trophies would be the trash barrel. They had been sent, they told Joop, to make sure that his stay was not only pleasant (here a new official from the Wildlife Bureau saluted) but also informative on the subjects in which he appeared to take an interest. They assumed this meant the forest ecosystem of the game preserve.

The little professor gave Joop a familiar, almost conspiratorial look, and the way his three colleagues were also staring fixedly from behind their spectacles aroused the suspicion in Joop that they might be out for blood. His blood, in fact. Could it be that these representatives of a new environmental school of thought had tracked him down in hopes of converting him? Finding the idea still amusing for the moment, he began to think of this foursome as his own private Furies, spirits who would sting his conscience with the persistence of horseflies.

After Joop had been shown to his room and had changed his clothes, the little group set out quickly for the forest in a horse-drawn wagon on which boards had been mounted in the back as seats. It was intended as a first excursion, without guns, to see whether they could spot any game before night fell. Since the official from the Wildlife Bureau spoke no German, he sat up front and chatted with the driver, while the Furies swarmed and buzzed around Joop in the rear. The humid afternoon heat was making him sleepy, but they kept after him—softly when the wagon was on level ground, and louder as it rumbled over ruts and potholes. Joop looked around as he rode, and saw a forest, but surprisingly few trees. They stood far apart here, and it was only the workings of the human eye, which pulls distant objects close together, that created the appearance of a dense forest. It was an optical illusion. And amid the hubbub as the environmentalists talked away at Joop, things began to flow together in his mind, sights mingling with sounds, new experiences with old beliefs, yesterday's certainty with today's doubts, words once read with spoken words and unspoken thoughts.

> Look, Mr. Joop, how the forest is dying
> Don't you see, Mr. Joop?
> It has gone gray on top and has no
> Children and grandchildren at its feet
> It is dying top and bottom at the same time
> Above the years are eating it up
> And down below the deer
> Two now four now six thousand of them in these
>   woods and in the blue forests where
>   The Drava meets the Danube
> A whole brothel of deer!
> Yes, Mr. Joop: a brothel! For it is here
> That the customers come from the West
> The fat cats with all the chins
> With big bellies and fat behinds
> With their big mouths and big cigars
> The big spenders—no offense, Mr. Joop!—
> Their fat wallets bulging in their pants
> And they get their kicks here, get off on
> Blowing away a prize stag
> At fifteen twenty thousand dollars a crack
> But the prize stag is only the top
> Of a broad-based pyramid of does and fawns
> And there are far too many pyramids here in the
>   woods
> And over there by the river and in the marshes
> Pyramids that the pharaoh is raising so that
> When one has its top blown away
> For fifteen or twenty thousand dollars
> There is another ready worth maybe

Twenty or twenty-five and then another worth
Why not thirty say thirty-five?
And the pharaoh feeds them all
Since the forest can't anymore
And with hormones too
Since nature is too sick to grow those
Twenty- or thirty-thousand-dollar antlers
By itself
And so it will go on until one day
These pyramids of deer will be standing alone
In a treeless desert
Like the pyramids of Egypt
Or if you prefer, Mr. Joop,
Since it is scientifically more accurate
In a treeless steppe like the one where
Cervus elaphus *first evolved*
But that will not mean nature has come full circle,
    Mr. Joop
Far from it
Nature will be dead and the people hungry
They will swallow up the pyramids and the pharaoh
    with them
And then the many chins
The big bellies and fat behinds
Won't come here anymore to empty their guns
Since the big mouths with their big cigars
Want a forest to go with the deer
Isn't that so, Mr. Joop
Because deer without a forest
Are about as appealing as a
Golf course with no grass
About as romantic as a lover whose hair
Falls out overnight
But the forest wasn't destroyed in a day
It grew thinner and thinner
Year after year
Losing its leaves on top
And its fertility below

But the romantics
The ones with the bulging pant pockets
Didn't see it coming
Because as long as these people have a forest
They don't see it
But when they don't have it anymore
Then they see
Do you see, Mr. Joop?

In the distance, fantastic herds of phantom stags were roaming through the gaping forest. Their antlers were short and thick, and it seemed as if they had kept them from growing on purpose for fear of becoming too conspicuous, as if they had channeled all their nourishment not into risky, gleaming points but into the squat stumps now covered in mossy vein-streaked velvet. It made the stags look alien, mysterious. With these pulsing weapons they were driving away the remaining daylight, so that night and peace would return to the forest. Then at last they could enter into a world of different human dreams, of dreams that didn't circle above their antlers like hungry vultures. When they threw their heads up in alarm, the clouds of flies around them rose and scattered. The swelling, piercing whine seemed to come from the herd, a united cry of pain.

Joop's head had dropped forward sleepily onto his chest. When he looked up, he found the four environmentalists smiling at him with knowing looks.

As had been agreed, they woke Joop at about four the next morning. Together, Joop, the official from the Wildlife Bureau, and the little professor, who came along as interpreter, climbed into a light hunting carriage drawn by two horses. Once again the official sat up front with the driver, while Joop and the professor rode in the back. No one felt like talking; between the end of the evening's activities and the early start there had been too few hours for sleep. With his rifle between his knees, Joop tried to rest his hands on the barrel and his chin on top of that, but the ride was too bumpy for anyone to doze off. The horses snorted softly, the carriage springs creaked, and the wheels squelched in the mud of the track. Now and then the driver and the official exchanged a few muttered words—probably about the route to take, Joop guessed. All he knew was that they were on the way to a blind where he would be able to shoot a particularly fine roebuck—*with the compliments of the Chief of State,* as the card handed to him the evening before had said.

After a short while they stopped at a forest ranger's station. Here their ways parted; the driver and the professor went into the cabin, while the man from the Wildlife Bureau led Joop on foot to a clearing about half a mile farther on. There the man pointed in the approximate direction from which Joop should expect the buck to emerge from the forest at first light. He made it clear that Joop should climb up and wait on the stand, and then he went away, leaving Joop alone. They had given him something to keep his legs warm, and the thought flashed through his mind that Mari would despise him twice over—once for using the blind, and once for the blanket! He stood his rifle in a corner. It was going to be a long wait.

The first rays of the sun were slicing through the trees when Joop saw the buck. He could see it clearly through his binoculars and was certain it was the animal he had been told about and given permission to shoot. Its massive size was unusual even for a male, and its coat was changing from winter gray to the deep red of summer. It looked about the right age, but most striking of all were the antlers, which extended from pronounced and deeply furrowed coronets to long forks, with the thickest branches Joop had ever seen on a living animal. He couldn't take his eyes off it, and caught up in his pleasure in looking at it he forgot to shoot. As the buck stood motionless, a ray of soft light filtered through the trees and struck its head, making its eyes shine like lumps of polished coal and turning its antlers so pale that the dark furrows stood out on them like living veins. Nothing moved at all except for the deer's nervously twitching penis; as the starting point from which life flows, it reminded Joop that he was here to end the life of this particular buck.

He quietly exchanged the binoculars for his rifle and centered the cross hairs on the animal's shoulder blade, behind which lay its heart. Then a sudden shiver ran through him. He had asked his doctor once about the shivers he sometimes got, for no apparent reason, that affected his shoulders, chest, and back. Now, absurdly inappropriately at such a precious moment, he recalled what the doctor had said: Sometimes the walls of the bladder will touch after it has been emptied, and that can send just such a shiver through a person. But it was not his bladder now, nor was it the effect of alcohol combined with too little sleep, the morning chill, or the usual butterflies in the stomach before making a shot. What had given him the tremors was the struggle going on inside him between disgust and desire. It was at Mari's tower that a new loathing for hunting trophies had taken hold of him; the excursion to the woods the day before had strengthened it. Now it contended against the old lust in the blood. From time immemorial this urge has always sought to purge itself through killing and mourning; nowadays, once it has been satisfied by enough shooting, it sometimes disguises itself as a good deed, the reestablishment of a lost natural balance between plants and animals. Both these feelings battled within Joop, desire and disgust, and some of the disgust came from his realization that hunters were attempting to escape public disapproval and smuggle their sport into the future by wrapping themselves in the cloak of progressive environmental thinking. But this new cloak did not quite succeed in hiding the old signs of lust on their bodies, signs that in simpler, more innocent times had never embarrassed them. This is what is ruining hunting, Joop said to himself, his thoughts becoming as cool and straight as the rifle stock against his cheek, not public opinion but the new motive of deception, and the resulting shame.

And so the shaking that had seized him had

something to do with the elimination of toxic substances, after all; it was just his mind being purged, he thought with sudden illumination, never letting his eye stray from the buck. But to his despair, in these moments containing the seeds of both life and death he couldn't tell which of the warring poisons was draining from him: the old desire or the new disgust.

Joop had shivered so violently that the rifle had slipped off his shoulder, deflecting his thoughts as well as his aim. A moment or so later he lowered the gun, letting the barrel rest on the railing, and sat transfixed, as if he and not the deer had just looked death in the face. Waiting for the buck to move on, he felt his eyes watering. He tried to tell himself they were tears of joy over the animal's escape, but he knew it wasn't so.

By the time he could see clearly again, the buck had vanished. Joop climbed down from the blind and trudged back to join the others. He told the official that he had never had a good shot at the deer; it was always standing at the wrong angle. The little professor translated, and when the incredulous official replied with a wordless shrug of his shoulders, the professor turned back and murmured softly, *'Atta boy,* smiling so inscrutably that it was impossible to tell what he meant by this phrase, which could have been used to praise a promising hunting dog who had responded well to its trainer. Did it refer to the fact that Joop had spared the deer's life, or to some presumed transformation, to a hope that he was now revolted by the idea of hunting for trophies? Perhaps it was only the mistake of a foreigner not in complete command of the language.

Joop was annoyed but said nothing. His thoughts were already elsewhere. They drove back to the hunting lodge. On Joop's program for the rest of the day was an excursion by boat through the marshes of the Danube and the Drava, with a chance to see cormorants, herons, and eagles. His audience with the great man was to follow.

The bear had stopped turning over stones. He wasn't that hungry anymore. But neither was he satisfied. And so he stayed on his feet when he finished the meal they had been giving him regularly for a week now, and went over the low bushes on the forest floor looking for more of last year's berries. He had to take care in these searches not to come too close to the clearing, for the places where he had been finding the meat put out for him in the last few days were not far from it.

One day he interrupted his grazing to lift his head and listen. The din of hammers and saws and the engines of the tractors and trucks they used to gather the cut logs and haul them away had grown familiar; he knew that these sounds faded between midday and evening and ceased completely before darkness fell. Now the bear moved noiselessly toward the unaccustomed stillness. When he reached the edge of the clearing, he cautiously pulled himself upright behind some of the fallen trees that remained, as he had done the day he attacked the charcoal maker. The scent of humans and the stink of their machines still lingered in the air, but as far as he could tell, the sources of these odors had left. The clearing lay empty. The bear did not bother with a closer inspection. It was enough for him that the noise had stopped earlier than usual and that the men were gone. They had taken their machines with them, too, something they had not done on the other evenings. He went back to where the meat had been left the day before, lay down in a nearby thicket, and waited for his daily meal. It arrived, just as it had every evening for a week. The bear didn't stop to think that by following the meat from place to place every day he was coming closer and closer to the clearing. Does a bear think at all? Probably not.

When he returned the following evening, as usual, prepared to follow the scent of the meat to the new site, he discovered that this time the meat lay at the edge of the clearing, between the last standing trees. It was not the same place he had gone to the day before to see why all the noise had stopped, however. At this spot nothing blocked his view of the open space; the bear would have no need to pull himself upright to see into it. As he arrived and laid one forepaw possessively on the fresh delivery of beef ribs, he could see down a broad corridor that had been completely cleared of dead wood. At the far end, about a hundred yards away, an object stood up against the edge of the forest as if on stilts, on four wooden tree trunks taller than even a tall bear standing upright. The bear couldn't make anything of it. He had never seen anything like it before. He had never seen death before, either, and now he was looking straight into its dark, empty eyes. But his heart didn't begin to pound. How could it have? If death comes instantaneously, for bears and their like it is no more than a momentary fright, the batting of an eye. It can't even be called a last fright, for are they capable of thinking, as it strikes them, *This is the end*?

The bear sank his teeth into the ribs. It wasn't his last meal; they weren't quite ready to execute him yet. But the executioners were gathered for their own feast.

Over an aperitif they inquired about one another's health. Over pheasant consommé with cheese croutons they reviewed the projects under consideration. Over grilled local fish with lemon butter and new potatoes they discussed the size of the loans, over saddle of venison with juniper sauce and Bohemian dumplings the term of the loans, over white chocolate mousse the interest rates, and over Turkish coffee the government's guarantees of political stability. Finally, when the ninety-year-old Armagnac was served, they got down to business. The dictator (present company excepted) took out of his wallet a set of before-and-after photos of a 12-point buck and passed them around the table. The assembled big-game hunters and top financiers assumed expressions of great seriousness. The antlers on the living animal were impressive enough; thanks to the camera angle, as a dead trophy they exceeded anything ever seen before. No doubt about it, proclaimed the dictator, it was a world record, and at the next world exhibition, which would probably be held in the West, it would do his country honor. Not only the country, said Joop, raising his glass in salute.

They moved into the next room to smoke. The Armagnac went well with the handmade Cuban cigars Fidel Castro sent at regular intervals to his *dear friend*. The clouds of blue smoke swirling under the lamps grew thicker and the mood of the party livelier as the guests stood in a circle around the great man, who suddenly had an idea. Calling over one of the servants, the dictator took hold of him by the arm and led him aside. To judge by the man's face, the instructions he was receiving were both unexpected and complicated. The dictator then returned to the group with a secretive smile and said nothing about what had just passed. Instead he expressed sympathy for Joop's unsuccessful attempt to get a buck the day before and, over Joop's polite protestations, promised to give him another go at something appropriately large for the occasion (without specifying just what the occasion was). At that moment the double doors to the room were flung open and four servants in green uniforms formed an honor guard for a fifth man, who entered bearing a large silver tray such as might be used to serve an elaborate ice-cream bombe. On the tray sat the decapitated head of the world-record buck, the sawed-off edges concealed

with white damask napkins and sprigs of evergreen. It had clearly just come out of a freezer: The
eyeballs were fogging up in the warmth of
the room. An invisible prop had been put under the
head to make the antlers point upward, as they had
in life, but this touch rendered the whole arrangement extremely unstable. When it began to list
dangerously to one side—a consequence of its
hasty preparation, no doubt—two members of the
honor guard quickly stepped up to lend a steadying
hand. Thus, to a smattering of applause from the
assembled company, the head reached the center of
the room and was set down on a small table hastily
pulled up to receive it.

Looking at it, Joop felt a wave of nausea. As the
eyes slowly cleared again, the animal appeared to
be coming back to life; Joop felt it was giving him
an unpleasantly questioning look, although he
couldn't have said what the question was. None of
the others noticed the changing eyes or their effect
on Joop; they were all occupied with the antlers.
Joop also felt nauseated by the slightly swollen and
protruding tongue, even though it was partly covered by a decorative sprig of evergreen—the traditional *last mouthful.*

He didn't participate in the expert appraisal of
the trophy, the reckoning of all its bony points, but
no one remarked on his silence, since the lively
discussion was being conducted in the local language. Finally the dictator gave a signal for the tray
to be taken away, and the conversation turned to
other matters. Joop felt better immediately. From

brief, intermittent translations he learned that they were talking about a bear, an unusually large animal, that must have wandered south from the Alps into a heavily wooded and mountainous area; it had never been sighted there before. It must also be extremely shy; up to now only two people had caught a glimpse of it: the game warden of the district and—here they all laughed heartily—some poor devil who had been making a charcoal kiln. The bear had seen him creeping about on all fours gathering wood and must have taken him for a wild pig. The man had been attacked but not killed, not even seriously injured, probably because he had played dead. No doubt each had been afraid of the other, or so the speculation ran. Now plans were being drawn up for how to deal with this bear; a commission had reported to His Excellency in the capital that it was old and dangerous, and since then the great man had been debating whether or not he ought to shoot it himself. It would be regarded as a great honor for the region.

A wild certainty was rising in Joop that he was about to receive an equal honor himself. It was accompanied by a furious blush that began in his face and spread down his neck and under his collar, as if the intense and contradictory emotions within him were fanning a fire. When the flush finally emerged from under his shirt cuffs onto his sweaty palms, he hid his hands in his jacket pockets. Everyone noticed, and no one said a word. The smoky haze drifted under the lamps like clouds announcing a change in the weather. Joop reached to undo the top button of his shirt but caught himself in time, thinking, *Not that! Anything but that!* It was a cry from the heart, and it was about more than how shirt collars should be worn. What Joop had once hoped for he now feared, certain of what he could not yet know. Suddenly the memory surfaced in his head of the evening when he had been immersed in work at home and the angry roar of a grizzly had washed over his unprepared mind.

The dictator had stopped and was smiling as if he had thought of something that pleased him; he looked at Joop all the while, and so fixedly that it was not difficult to guess what he was about to say. Everyone there did guess. He looked just the way The People imagined their leader looked at moments of grave decision, like a man with the welfare of the nation closest to his heart. But it is doubtful that his heart was in it when he offered the bear to Joop.

The bear found his next piece of meat lying directly in the corridor that ran across the clearing. This path was twenty yards wide and still bordered on both sides by trees brought down by the storm; at its far end, where the forest began again, stood the hunting blind. The man who came and went with the bear's daily meal had become an unquestioned element of the swinish well-being that now radiated from the animal's guts day after day; apart from him, the bear had seen no more humans since the woodcutters' departure, and so he forgot about them. The blind, where nothing ever moved, seemed to him no more than a peculiar arrangement of tree trunks, and like all the other peculiar patterns of trees knocked down by the storm, it reminded him of nothing he had ever known that spelled danger. And so he forgot about it, too. He had even stopped paying attention to the arrival of the man with the meat; all that concerned him was the man's departure, since this signaled to the bear that he could heave himself out of his hiding place and set off for another undisturbed meal. He took his time, for there was no reason to hurry now. One evening, after making a large meal of root tubers during the day, he had even been tempted to stay in his den and pass up the meat, but then he went after all. After a long day that had been more tiring than refreshing, gluttony (which was in part also curiosity about whether there might not be a new kind of meat he had never tasted before) and boredom overcame his well-fed lethargy in the end. And so he forgot about everything: first people, then the shooting stand, and finally a lifetime's worth of vigilance and suspicion.

For one night and a whole day before the night that was to be the bear's last, the meat bringer failed to appear. When the bear had grown tired of waiting, he left his thicket and searched up and down the whole corridor from one end to the other, including under the blind, but found no meat anywhere. Since he was already there, he inspected the stand, sniffing at the stilts and even pulling himself upright on the ladder at its back. But he found only one scent on all the wood; it was of humans, but old. So he started back down the corridor toward the forest with a low growl, shaking his head in a way that is typical of bears but that in this instance could have been taken as an expression of bewilderment. He took his small but growing appetite with him to his den under the uprooted spruce tree.

We must let him get good and hungry, Dushan said to Joop. He was explaining his feeding strategy. Their feelings on seeing each other again had been friendly and almost warm, given the limits imposed by their different nationalities and vastly different social status. Dushan's German was sufficient for hunting purposes, and constantly improving through his work guiding German hunters to roebucks, stags, and the odd bear.

Joop had been asked to come to the headquarters of the government in the provincial capital, since that was where Dushan's supervisors had their offices. As a guest of the head of state, Joop had been received with the kind of courtesy that borders on servility and is motivated not so much by a desire to honor the guest as by a cringing fear of those higher up. Joop had also been visited by the commission that had reported to the national capital the events surrounding the bear. They had come to his hotel, where there had been more repellent speeches of welcome in the lobby, accompanied by the inevitable toasts; at least the schnapps was honest, thought Joop. When the conversation came round to the bear, Joop uttered two requests, which his determined tone made sound more like conditions, that astonished his hosts and forestalled all objections: First, he wished to have his old guide again, whose first name was Dushan; unfortunately he couldn't remember any more (Joop kept quiet about his problem with the consonants). And second, he insisted on paying the precise sum the bear would have cost him if he had booked it through the state Tourist Bureau, as usual. (Did I really say *booked*? Joop wondered.) He asked them to name the price, the full price, please; they should make no reduction and certainly not try to change his mind. He could tell from the expressions on their faces, he added, that they would like to, and no doubt felt it was their duty, but in this case he would have to insist. Joop gave no reason for his adamancy about paying, but it was clear to everyone there that a representative of the World Bank would want to accept no favors that might compromise his independence.

To arrange for Dushan as a guide was no problem, they told Joop; as the game warden of the district, he would have been sent in any case. But as for taking money from their distinguished visitor, that was a different matter altogether, and might cause displeasure. The invitation had come from the very highest levels, after all; they would have to inquire. Joop replied that he would merely leave a check and, to end the discussion, added that the matter could be decided later. This seemed acceptable to the commission. Turning away from them with a banker's tact, Joop wrote out a check for the sum that, with some trepidation, they had finally named: thirty-five thousand dollars. Then Dushan was called, and their meeting took place as described, without any sense of arrogance or servility on either side. Both Joop and Dushan were hunters now, no more and no less, and they set out together that same evening for the charcoal maker's clearing.

Dushan had a horse with him, a small animal already gray in the face; its coat was rough and bristly, and it looked miserably underfed. Tied onto its back was a large sack that hung down on both sides; it contained Dushan's equipment, two blankets, and, since it was going to be a long night, some food. They had their rifles out, slung over their shoulders, for they were already in dangerous country. Joop wondered for a brief moment why the horse wasn't carrying any meat for the bear, but he said nothing and then forgot about it. In any case they soon stopped speaking altogether, partly because Dushan's German was not good enough to answer any detailed questions, and partly because they were approaching their quarry's territory.

A last exchange took place when they came to an underpass tunneling beneath a highway; here the level ground ended, rising on the other side to a harvested cornfield with a forest-covered mountainside above it. Dushan had found the bear's paw prints here and knew from them where the bear had gone into the forest. Joop suddenly asked him the name of the district through which this highway ran, as if something had just occurred to the German; to Dushan's surprise, Joop even asked him to spell it. After that they did not speak again. Joop became preoccupied with certain thoughts, as the path running up the mountain along the edge of the forest demanded little attention. The night was clear and starry, with the moon approaching full. Dushan walked at the horse's head, with Joop following behind.

The wave of heat Joop felt coming over him could not have been caused by the effort of the climb, since the path was only moderately steep. It came instead from the suspicion, now bordering on certainty, that his fate had been linked with this bear for a long time now, long before he realized it.

He had learned something of the bear's history from the authorities in the provincial capital, and apparently it had come from a neighboring country. According to reports, one of the remote Alpine valleys there had been home to a solitary bear for many years, but it had disappeared about the time work began on a large dam. They mentioned the name of the valley to Joop, and no one had had to spell it for him; he was one of the top people involved in financing the whole development scheme. The highway that cut the bear's current territory in two had also crossed his desk, at least in its financial aspects, and he had only recently finished inspecting and approving a plan to extend it. But that wasn't all. He remembered plans they had told him about for making use of the highway. By linking this Eastern country to the capitalist

West, the highway would open up export markets for the national logging industry; all they needed was to build better roads and buy heavy equipment for moving the timber. When New York had asked his opinion about granting loans for this, Joop's response had been favorable; he had argued that going ahead with this project would go a long way toward recovering previous loans. The documents had also contained detailed proposals for increasing tourism as well as lumber-industry activity in the forests; they could develop certain sites for weekend and seasonal rentals, for instance, build playgrounds and climbers' shelters, lay out hiking paths and barbecue areas. Other suggestions included forest preserves with adjacent parking lots as further possibilities for improving the infrastructure. Joop remembered the latter particularly well, since he had purposely avoided taking a stand on them. The sector of the German press devoted to hunters and their concerns had informed him thoroughly about the negative effects on wild game of tourists tramping through the woods.

Now and then Joop was inclined to express a thought in a pointed, almost epigrammatic fashion. And since it was approaching midnight, it was also time to end the day with a true thought, a principle that applied not only when he was in bed. And so he thought: *You have already killed this bear, even before you shoot it.*

He yanked at his collar impatiently, almost ripping it open, and twisted his sweaty neck back and forth; the gesture not only reflected a new way of thinking in his outward behavior, but also sent a rush of fresh blood to his brain: *this pretentious, overdecorated rifle on his shoulder, shimmering in the starlight, his special hunting clothes, the best money could buy, his rucksack of velvety deerskin, dyed green to match, the silver flask in his breast pocket, filled with specially aged Swiss eau-de-vie, the Cuban cigars in his rucksack, each in its own silver casing, the gold and silver stickpins on his Tyrolean hat, and the tired and miserable horse stumbling along ahead of him, Dushan's worn and shabby clothes, his rucksack up there on the horse's back, stinking and full of holes, his cheap schnapps in an old soda bottle, the soggy cigarettes he rolled himself, his greasy old cap askew on his head . . .*

None of this fit together, it matched neither the time nor the place, and all his elegant and expensive merchandise was worth nothing without Dushan up front, Dushan with his grubby gear and miserable, tired, stumbling horse. Without Dushan he would never be able to find what he was looking for, never see what he was seeing; the gold trim on his rifle would not make him less helpless in the woods, the eau-de-vie would not save him from desperation. Nothing fit anything, thought Joop, nothing was good for anything, everything was so painfully out of place, so pretentious. He had valued the tools more than the craft, the objects more than their use. He had valued appearances more than reality.

Joop was in a mental state bordering on panic,

as he had been on approaching Mari's stone pheasant, when he hadn't been able to decide whether to turn off or not and had let the chauffeur drive past the entrance. Now he was debating whether he shouldn't give up the whole idea of hunting this bear, and even began to run through the details in his mind of how he would manage to save face: He would pretend to have a heart attack, fake groans as he rode back on the horse, reach his car and driver waiting near Dushan's village, and set out for the border at once. He realized what a chaotic, even ridiculous frame of mind he was in only when he caught himself making the excuse that there was no room on the walls at home for a bearskin, and that he probably wouldn't even like having one there anyway. This tipped the balance the other way. He thought of the German Museum of Hunting in Munich; they could display it, and he could show his friends what his expensive rifle could do. With this idea and an unsteady grip on the horse's sticky tail, Joop managed to pull himself out of the chaos raging in his head.

Just as they were about to enter the forest, a man came out of its shadow to meet them. Joop reacted with a frightened start, but then he recalled what Dushan had told him about the need to deceive the bear. This must be the man, the game warden of the neighboring district who had been sent over to make sure the bear didn't stay away. As far as Joop could see, this man resembled Dushan in every respect: shabby clothing, cloth cap, cigarette dangling from the corner of his mouth, and the old

German carbine from World War II over his shoulder. Dushan murmured something by way of introduction; they shook hands briefly and moved on into the woods. The new man fell into line behind Joop, and before the shadows swallowed them up Joop had regained enough of his normal humor to be amused at the picture they made. It ought to be called "Two Revolutionaries Leading Away a Member of the Ruling Class in Hunting Dress," he thought to himself.

Toward two o'clock in the morning they arrived at the charcoal maker's clearing. Joop thought he might have overexerted himself on the long climb through the forest, which had been rough going in the dark, and was concerned about the steadiness of his aim. Fear rose in him that he might humiliate himself by missing or, even worse, by only wounding the bear, who would be able to escape into the woods and disappear. He inhaled deep lungfuls of the pine-scented night air to try to calm his racing pulse.

Then something happened that caught Joop off guard and threw him completely off balance, although if he had given it any thought he would have seen it coming: Dushan killed the horse, which had been intended all along as the fresh bait for the bear. While the other man took the halter and stroked its head (something that had probably not happened often in the old creature's lifetime, but was all the more falsely affectionate now at the moment of its death), Dushan held a mechanism between its ears of the kind butchers once used in slaughterhouses, and pulled the trigger. Simultaneously with a sharp click the horse fell to the ground with a metal pin in its brain. A moment later Joop saw the glint of a long knife in the moonlight and turned his head away. He walked the twenty paces to the stand and climbed up the ladder at the back. When he sat down on the bench and looked through the sighthole, he saw a small fat cloud rising above the slaughtered horse's neck in the cold night air. He shivered.

The two men were in a hurry; they knew the bear was not far off and had included his fast of the previous day in their calculations; it was difficult for them to predict how he would react to the warm blood and the unaccustomed amount of meat on the carcass. Since Joop was already seated in the blind, they both climbed up to join him. The third man, who was now supposed to trick the bear by leaving, approached Joop to say good-bye, according to Dushan, but the truth was that he was hoping for a tip. Joop pulled from his pocket the hundred-mark bill he had put there for just this reason; he knew the rules of the game. Whether in disbelief or suspicion is hard to say, but the man put his hand with the bill in it through the slit of the blind into the moonlight; when he had made out the number on it, he pulled it back in with a delighted word of thanks. Joop pretended not to see the hand offered him to shake, hoping the slight could be excused as unintended in the darkness of the blind. He felt somehow unclean. The words *blood money* flashed through his mind, and also the thought that the shame fell on him. He was glad to see the man go. Joop and Dushan heard him making a noisy job of it on purpose, stumbling up against logs and stones and even whistling a few bars. On no account was the bear to miss the man's departure; that might make him also miss the bait.

Uncertain about whether there will be meat today or none again like yesterday, the bear doesn't stir from his den under the uprooted spruce tree. The forest remains quiet long into the night. Then he hears footsteps, but they are far away and not accompanied by any information for his nose; the wind is coming from the wrong direction. All the same, he crawls out of his cave, shakes the dirt from his fur, and yawns so hugely that his jaws crack with a sound like a tree branch breaking. And he takes his time setting out to look for the bait he hopes to find. When he finally goes, it is without haste, and as noiselessly as if he were touching the ground with down cushions and not with four feet the size of great loaves of bread, with claws on the ends.

It takes the bear some time to reach the charcoal maker's clearing. A fog wafts toward him, growing thicker the closer he gets to the cleared corridor. It is a greasy fog. It is full of blood. It is a meaty fog. It is a fog thick enough to sink his teeth into, and the bear does, pulling it into his lungs at the same time, thinning it with his saliva; it is that thick now that the bear is standing at the end of the corridor, which lies in deadly silence before him with the carcass in it, the carcass that has created this heady brew. In the distance, the footsteps of the man who brought the meat are fading away. The bear sighs—never mind the people who will tell you a bear doesn't sigh. It is a sigh of desire; he can't hold back his saliva or his legs, which start to run with him as if they were carrying his desire alone, and not his heavy body. At the carcass he makes a ridiculous spectacle of himself; he mistimes how long it will take him to stop and slips in the horse's blood, landing suddenly on his rump on the bare, clayey ground that has been torn up by the logging trucks. He sits there like a huge, clumsy teddy bear with his legs out in front of him, sticky with blood. Blood lies in small puddles all around the carcass. The bear laps at them with his tongue, but soon stops. Lapping up blood won't fill the stomach of any bear, let alone a large one. And so he digs his teeth into the horse's belly, to get at its guts, blind and deaf and mute and stupid with greed. This is how Joop's bullet hits him.

It comes out of a burst of light so bright that it blinds not only the marksman and his quarry but also the moon, which pulls a cloud over its face. It comes out of a burst of noise, too, that deafens the bear with its shock and makes him oblivious to the pain in his shattered left shoulder. And all of this, the flash of light, the crashing noise, the shock, and the smashed shoulder, was accomplished by the pressure of one fingertip, so slight a pressure that if an ant had crept in between Joop's finger and the trigger of his rifle, it would not have been crushed, not even injured. The hair rose on the back of Joop's neck; Mari was standing behind him, saying: *That makes us look bad!*

The bullet he had meant for the bear's heart had passed just above it and exited below the bottom left rib, and after ripping a hole in the bear's belly it did the same to the horse carcass, mingling the green slime from the one with the red blood of the other. Blood trickles and drips and spurts a little now in the rhythm of the bear's heartbeats. Above this the shock ebbs in long waves. They pulse against the inside of his skull and flood his eyes with red pain. An undirected rage fills the bear, and it roars from him. The sound splits the night and wakes the wind, sending it rushing through the trees. Before the next scream he stands up, ramrod straight with his head lifted and mouth open to roar again. His left foreleg dangles at his side like an empty windsock; he lifts the other toward the shooting stand and staggers forward a few steps. Joop sees it, hears the bear cry out: *What are you doing to me?* But the bear has not cried out; his cry exists only in Joop's head. He has even stopped roaring, his voice drowned in the blood pouring from his burst lung past his vocal cords and into his mouth. He is chewing on himself now.

In this stance his chest is facing Joop, who is overwhelmed with grief. It is time to end this *execution*, he thinks. He searches for the heart in the cross hairs, draws a deep breath, stops breathing, and applies the tiny weight of his finger to the gold-plated trigger. He can't see what happens next in the glare of the explosion. But he knows what is happening inside the bear: A shock wave is passing through the body fluids ahead of the bullet, ripping apart blood vessels and nerves. On the bullet's way to the heart, the soft lead around its tip mushrooms out, doubling the caliber of the hard core.

And as if that were not enough to kill, one part of the projectile flies into tiny splinters that rip apart the large muscles of the bear's chest and back. What is left of Joop's bullet pierces the heart and turns sideways, as if exhausted by the organ's vital force, but it still has enough energy to blast open a crater in the bear's back as big as the palm of your hand, sending blood bubbling out like lava. Once again the night air is filled with small greasy clouds.

Long before Joop has time even to think all this, however, the bear has collapsed on top of the horse carcass, dead. Joop bares his head. Dushan shakes Joop's hand and passes him the bottle of schnapps. Joop murmurs an embarrassed, insincere *thank you* and takes a swig. But it is not the cheap spirits that send a shudder through him, shaking him until he grows rigid, his eyes staring, mute. Dushan registers Joop's distress without understanding it. He departs. Joop stays on alone in the blind until the moon finally departs, too. The night wind runs its fingers gently through the bear's fur.

Three weeks later—he had long since returned to his desk and the Bay of Pigs—Joop received a letter from the Wildlife Bureau in the region of the Eastern European country where he had gone on his hunt. He felt distinctly uncomfortable as he opened it, although he had nothing to fear (they will simply be notifying him of his trophy, the bearskin). It was just that he would rather not be reminded of the whole episode. He was back in flannel again, back in charcoal gray.

He had purposely buried himself in work on his return, to the point that he had almost succeeded not in forgetting the bear's execution—that would be impossible—but in repressing it. *Execution*—to his dismay this word has stuck in him like a barbed hook; he cannot think of the killing without feeling it stab his conscience. The word is like a title under the picture of the bear's dreadful end. Since he can't get it out of his head, especially at night, when he has to pass his gun rack in the hall on the way to the bathroom, he has taken refuge in the kind of cynicism that always cheered him up after even the most questionable deals or love affairs. This cynical motto ran: *I paid my money and I got what I paid for, that's all.* He paid for the bear and now he will get its skin—any objections? Money has been his tried and true method of straightening out the things that went wrong in his life; it has always worked.

The letter opened with congratulations on the fine success of his kill and went on to announce that the measurements and evaluation of the trophy by the responsible commission had resulted in an unusually high number of points; in fact the total approached the world record for *Ursus arctos Linné,* the European brown bear. For this reason the skin fell into a category where, in the national interest, export was prohibited. They regretted to inform him that they would thus not be able to send it to him as expected. They did plan to exhibit it in a museum devoted to hunting, however, in a glass case suitable for so valuable an object, and with his kind permission a brass plate would be mounted on it to inform the public of the place and date of the kill as well as of Joop's name. In view of their inability to release the trophy, he would of course be reimbursed in full for the hunter's fee he had paid; he would find his uncashed check enclosed, and they looked forward to seeing him again in the future . . . et cetera.

Joop dropped the letter onto his desk blotter with a gesture that suggested helplessness. When he picked up the envelope, to see where it had been sent from, his check fell out and drifted to the floor so slowly that Joop felt it was mocking him. He couldn't very well leave it lying there, and so he had to bend down and pick up the money he couldn't seem to get rid of, the money that had begun to soothe and heal his injured conscience. Angrily he tore up the check and thrust the pieces into his trouser pocket, the safest depository for masculine insecurities.

Three days later, Joop gave instructions to a moving company to come get the painting of Diana from his office and ship it to Mari in the United States. And on the same day he hired a man to install a glass pane with a lock on the front of his gun rack in the hall. The man recommended museum glass.